Seaside
Gifts

D1563059

GAYLE ROPER

ISBN: 1-942265-07-7
ISBN-13: 978-1942265078

CHAPTER ONE

Every time Nan Patterson surveyed the aisles of Present Perfect, she stared potential failure in the face. Depending on the moment, she was either terrified or energized by her gift shop on the boardwalk in Seaside, a barrier island off the coast of New Jersey. Some days, she was both.

At the moment, one thirty on a June Monday afternoon, she felt good about how things were going. Two women were walking around the store with don't-bother-me-I'm-shopping expressions on their faces, a delight for a store owner to see. A third had just bought five sparkly rings with different colored stones.

"One for each of my four grand-girls," she'd said. "And one for me." With a satisfied smile she walked toward the door that exited to the boardwalk.

A cop entered and moved toward the rear of the store, approaching Nan. His hands rested on his belt, which had all the cop paraphernalia hanging from it, as if holding on would prevent him from bumping into anything as he passed through the aisles.

Men were frequently uncomfortable in the shop. Large bodies and breakable items were a bad match. Add the cop's belt, and it was a disaster waiting to happen. At least the cop seemed to think so.

He was good looking, tall, and broad shouldered with a careful smile he directed at her as she stood behind the cash register. If she could have chosen someone to respond to her call about the crime, she couldn't have done better.

He stepped aside to make room for the woman who was admiring one of the five new sparkly rings shining on her right hand. Her shopping bag with the remaining rings wasn't large, but she was, and the cop visibly inhaled to try and make himself thinner as she passed.

It was a very tight squeeze.

When the woman had moved successfully down the aisle, he exhaled and looked around, taking in Present Perfect's eclectic stock. He eyed the colorful cards, placemats and napkins in sherbet shades, nice though inexpensive jewelry, small ceramic and wooden figurines, framed and unframed prints and photographs of landscapes and seascapes, wooden signs that read SEASIDE in different scripts and colors, clever little lighthouses, pretty plates bearing beach scenes, and her favorite part of the shop, the Christmas corner.

Nan could easily interpret his expression: *Who wants all this stuff?* And when he scowled at the Christmas tree, he was clearly wondering who buys Christmas stuff in June. Poor guy. He'd be so much happier at The Home Depot with its wide aisles and power tools.

He finally reached the counter and almost sighed with relief.

"I'm looking for your boss."

Nan liked the deep voice that went with the deep brown eyes. "You're talking to her." Being a mere wisp over five feet and slim as a boy always made people look around for the boss.

He raised an eyebrow. "Nan Patterson?"

"That's me." She held out her hand. "Thanks for coming so quickly."

He swallowed his surprise and gave a brief, professional shake. "Well, theft is a serious thing."

She frowned. "What theft?"

He looked disconcerted and pulled a small notebook from his pocket. He flipped a few pages until he came to what he wanted. He pointed as if she could see what was written there. "Didn't you call about thievery?"

"Oh!" She gave him her best grin. "Not thievery. Leavery."

It was his turn to look blank.

"Leavery," Nan repeated. "Someone keeps leaving things here."

She could see—she squinted at his chest and read his name tag—Officer Eastman lose interest. It was as obvious as a balloon deflating as it lost its air.

"I'm sure whoever left whatever will return for it." He gave a polite smile while clearly communicating that the Seaside PD wasn't in the lost and found business. His hands went to his belt as he prepared to turn and face the gauntlet of narrow aisles once again.

"No, no," Nan said hastily. "It's not like someone leaving a purchase or an umbrella or something. Someone is leaving valuable items."

"Then all the more reason they'll come for them."

There might as well have been a blinking neon sign over his head. *False alarm. Waste of time.*

She leaned toward him as if proximity would make him understand. "Not purchased items. Abandoned items. Valuable abandoned items."

He frowned. "Abandoned items." He clearly didn't get it.

"Like a Limoges cup and saucer or a Royal Doulton figurine or an antique doll."

Nan chose to see his frown as an improvement over the disinterest of a moment ago. She reached under the counter and carefully pulled out a white china pitcher with gold vines all over it, clusters of raised golden grapes nestled amid the vines. "Unique Wedgwood."

"Uh-huh." He continued to look unimpressed.

Nan reminded herself that they didn't study fine china at the Police Academy. She tried again. "This isn't part of the stock of Present Perfect. I don't carry things of this quality. The boardwalk is hardly the venue for really good stuff."

Food, sunglasses, beach towels, and Seaside T-shirts and sweatshirts were the staples of most shops, except for Present Perfect, which attracted its customers by offering an alternative. Still, it was the boardwalk, and pricey was out.

He glanced around the store again and seemed to understand that while everything she had was lovely in its own way, it was also far from expensive.

"This pitcher appeared this morning." She held it up for him to see. "It's like *poof!* There it was."

He looked at it, then at her, and blinked.

She bit back a sigh at his lack of comprehension. "I opened the store, walked next door to grab a coffee, and when I got back, there it was, sitting on a counter beside some pretty plastic luncheon plates with matching glasses." She ran a gentle finger over a grape cluster. "This baby is worth about $50 if eBay is any indication. Not a great sum, but still, it's totally different from my stock."

She put it back beneath the counter. "Someone just left it, and I have no idea who. Or why. The Royal Doulton Balloon Man and Balloon Woman appeared yesterday. A Limoges cup and saucer appeared two days ago, as did a small original watercolor of a Ferris wheel. Left with no explanation. The first thing appeared about a week ago, a doll with a bisque head. She was left propped against the cash register."

Officer Eastman's face lit up. "Leavery."

Finally! "That's why I called the police. I don't know what to do about it."

"Say thank you?" Officer Eastman suggested.

Nan narrowed her eyes. "Cute."

He grinned, which made her glare harder. "I want to give the stuff back, but I don't know who to give it to or how to go about finding who to give it to. You guys solve mysteries."

A customer came to the counter, eyeing Officer Eastman uncertainly. Nan immediately abandoned him and smiled at her customer, who held a small silver picture frame with pressed flowers under its glass.

"Lovely, isn't it?" Nan said as she took the frame. "The woman who does this work is a Seaside resident."

"Really?" The customer opened her large multi-colored beach bag, rummaged for a while, and finally pulled out a credit card. "That makes it an even better memento of our vacation."

Nan swathed the picture in tissue and used a piece of tape to hold the wrappings in place. She pulled out one of the distinctive royal blue bags with Present Perfect written in gold across it, the lettering a miniature version of the sign Aunt Char had hung out front thirty years ago when she opened the place.

The customer pointed vaguely to one corner of the shop. "You have a wonderful antique bugle over there. I'd love to get it for my husband. He belonged to a bugle corps in high school, but there's no price on it."

Nan didn't think her manner faltered, but Officer Eastman narrowed his eyes and looked where the woman indicated.

"I'm sorry," Nan said with the warmest smile she could manage. "If there's no price tag, the item isn't for sale. It's just for atmosphere. Interest. Amusement."

The woman was not amused.

Nan kept her smile in place as she ran the card for the dried flower picture and collected the customer's signature. She even managed to stay behind the counter until the woman left the store. Then she bolted for the corner.

Sure enough, an old brass bugle, tarnished and dinged, sat on the counter between a display of lovely floral notepaper—some of her older customers still wrote letters—and a trio of ornate picture frames holding the beautiful faces of models looking delighted with life.

Officer Eastman peered over her shoulder. "Not part of your stock?"

Nan shook her head. "I've never seen it before." She turned and blinked at how close he was, and he took a quick step back.

"I can take this in and have it checked for prints—"

"Yes!" What a good idea. Very NCIS. And he did look a little like Tony DiNozzo.

"—but I doubt there would be a match in the system. Someone who starts leaving things instead of taking them isn't a good candidate for a police record."

Nan sighed. She didn't want logic, she wanted answers. "When I found the pitcher this morning, I hoped that would be it for the day. But no, now there are two things."

"Somebody's being twice as nice?" He gave a little half smile, as if he could charm her out of her grump, which he undoubtedly could if she weren't so frustrated with him.

"Don't you get it?" She shook the bugle at him. "The leavery is escalating!"

CHAPTER TWO

Roger Eastman got it all right, on two levels. One, she had a problem she didn't know how to solve, and she expected the police, namely him, to have the answer. And two, he thought she was one of the cutest things he'd seen in a long time, especially when her pretty hazel eyes narrowed as she all but snarled at him in frustration. Very unprofessional of him to find her agitation so endearing, but he did. And she was such a little thing. All his protective instincts kicked into high gear, but he reminded himself to step back and think of Lori.

That killed any attraction he felt. He was all professional.

He nodded and looked as serious as he could manage. "The leavery is escalating. I see what you mean."

"Do you?" Her hands went to her hips and she glared at him, the bugle in her hand threatening to knock over the picture on the counter behind her. "I think you think this whole situation is a joke."

He sighed. She was so cute when she snarled, like a Lab puppy trying to sound fierce. *Lori. Lori. Lori.* "Well, if these items are stolen—"

She sputtered with outrage. "You think I stole these things?"

"—which I assume they aren't, at least not by you, or you wouldn't have called, then something strange is going on."

She gritted her teeth, probably so she wouldn't shout. "Ya think?"

He flipped his notebook to an empty page. "So let's consider the alternatives."

She nodded, her expression saying it was about time. Then she forgot him as another customer approached the register with a box holding a Christmas tree ornament in one hand and several ornaments hanging from the fingers of the other.

"Did you find everything you were looking for?" Nan asked, the soul of good cheer as she stepped behind her counter.

Rog looked at the collection of angels, glittery stars, and colorful balls as, one by one, the woman unhooked them from her fingers and handed them to Nan. He caught sight of a nine-dollar price tag hanging from one angel. Granted it was pretty, but couldn't she find a whole box of similar angels at half the price at Walmart?

"These are so unique," the woman gushed. "I love them."

Apparently not.

"Only this one doesn't have a price." She held out the box which contained a white ball with a painted scene on it, a green bow reading Wedgwood tied to the top.

Nan barely blinked, but Rog's antennae pinged to alert. Another leavery item.

"I'm sorry," Nan told her customer. She gave a smile of such wattage Rog was surprised he and the lady weren't blinded. "I don't know how that got in the display."

"It's a Wedgwood Twelve Days of Christmas ball," the customer said. "It's Day One. See the partridge?"

Rog leaned in. Sure enough, a colorful partridge nestled into the white ceramic ball.

"There are two others from the same collection over there," the customer said helpfully. "Four calling birds and twelve drummers drumming. I suppose they aren't for sale either? I was going to get them too, if they didn't cost an obscene amount."

"Sorry." Nan put the ball in its box beneath the counter with, if he remembered correctly, a Wedgwood pitcher. Clearly someone liked Wedgwood, yet gave it away.

The customer sighed. "That's okay. They're probably out of my price range anyway."

While the customer and Nan completed their business, Rog googled Wedgwood Christmas balls and blinked. The partridge was going for almost $400, the calling birds, $370, and the drummers, $240. A dinged bugle—who gave away a dinged bugle?—was one thing, but items worth a thousand dollars were a totally different matter.

When the customer left with her bulging bag of tissue-wrapped tree ornaments, Rog asked Nan, "Can you leave the counter in someone else's care so we can talk without interruption?"

Nan looked at her watch. "I'm here alone right now. Tammy's due in about fifteen minutes. We'll have to wait for her." She squinted up at him. "You don't happen to know anyone who would like a summer job, do you? I have another girl who comes in from three to close, but I need someone else for, say, eleven to nine."

Did he know someone? He just might. He'd have to check.

He opened his mouth to tell her he might be able to help her when a voice called out, "Hello, Nan, my sweet."

Rog turned to see a little old lady in a bright pink knit top and navy knee-length shorts trotting down the aisle. A wrinkled and tanned hand clutched the handle of a large red cloth bag dangling from her shoulder, and her white Reeboks were so new they almost sparkled. Her most interesting feature was her red hair, a very unusual shade for a woman her age, though it was somehow attractive, even if it did clash with her bright pink shirt.

"Aunt Bunny." With a smile, Nan came from behind the counter and gave the old woman a hug. "How are you today?"

"Doing well." Aunt Bunny patted Nan's cheek in a proprietary way. "Don't you love this

warm weather?" She grinned up at Rog, her good humor shining from her eyes. "Keeps my arthritis at bay."

What was he supposed to say to that? Good? Or would she think he meant it was good she had arthritis?

"Aunt Bunny, this is Officer Eastman," Nan said. "He's come about the items that have been left."

"Nice to meet you, young man." Aunt Bunny held out her hand, the wattle of skin beneath her arm swaying with the movement. "I'm Bunny Truscott. I hope you're taking good care of my Nan."

"Pleased to meet you, ma'am." He shook her hand, surprised at the strength of the grip. She might be little and old, but she was fit.

"Look what I found today, Aunt Bunny." Nan pulled out the pitcher, the tree ornament, and the bugle.

Mrs. Truscott studied them with interest. "Lovely, aren't they?"

"Of course," Nan said. "Except for the bugle. Why a beat up bugle when everything else is so elegant?" She waved her hand as if waving away the words. "But that's not the point."

"Maybe lovely is the point. I think you should just enjoy them." She turned to Rog. "Don't you?"

"Aunt Bunny, they're not mine!"

Mrs. Truscott ran a hand over the pitcher. She picked it up and read the bottom. "Wedgwood. Huh. Not the usual dignified style, though it's lovely in its own garish way. Don't you think?" She looked at Rog again.

"You like Wedgwood, Mrs. Truscott?" Rog asked.

Nan shot him a dirty look, as if she thought he suspected Aunt Bunny. Which he supposed he did. He suspected everyone. It went with being a cop.

Mrs. Truscott looked at him in surprise. "Doesn't everyone love Wedgwood?"

Rog had no idea. His mother didn't. At least she didn't own any that he knew of, but with five sons, china knickknacks weren't the wisest things to display.

"If that last customer was right, there are more ornaments." Nan went to the Christmas corner. When she returned, she held out both hands, each holding a boxed white ceramic tree ball.

"I've got to tell you, this is the most unusual case I've ever worked." Rog peered at the ornaments, wondering if Nan had any idea of the value of the items she held.

"Really?" Mrs. Truscott looked at him in surprise. "I thought cops saw all kinds of weird things."

"Oh, we do, but they're usually terrible, sad, nasty. This is—" He searched for a word.

"Nice?" Mrs. Truscott suggested.

Rog laughed. "I guess you could say that."

"No, you couldn't," Nan said. "I'm just waiting for someone to come along and accuse me of stealing."

Mrs. Truscott patted Nan's hand but spoke to Rog. "I keep telling her this is a store. She should just sell whatever shows up if she doesn't want to keep it. Consider it extra inventory. Or if she likes some things, she can keep them. Consider them grace-gifts."

"Grace-gifts?"

"You know," Mrs. Truscott said. "Like God's grace. Undeserved. Unearned. Freely given. Like His love, His acceptance, and His salvation."

Nan spread her arms wide in the classic I-can't-believe-it gesture. "But they aren't mine!"

"I don't know who else's they'd be," Mrs. Truscott said. "They're presents for you. Presents for Present Perfect."

Nan's finger stabbed the air. "Gifts come from someone you know, and you know why you got them, even if it's just because the giver felt like giving. But these? Who knows?"

Mrs. Truscott pursed her lips. "I see what you mean. Well, I haven't an answer unless it's what you said. The giver just feels like giving."

Rog frowned. "I don't know, Mrs. Truscott. There's got to be a reason someone is leaving these things."

The old lady resettled her red bag on her shoulder. "Isn't *just because* a reason? I like to give things just because."

Really? Just because? Every gift he'd ever given or received was for a specific reason—like birthdays or Christmas. He'd never gotten one just because, nor had he given one just because. He suddenly suspected that was a guy thing, and he'd just stumbled on another of the myriad ways women were different from men.

Mrs. Truscott waved her hand like she was waving aside the leavery discussion. "Before I forget why I came, Nan, my sweet, I'm inviting you for dinner."

"Oh. How nice." There was a noticeable hesitance in Nan's voice, which surprised Rog.

Mrs. Truscott heard the caution too—and laughed. "I'm not cooking. I'm sending out."

Nan smiled and said with wholehearted enthusiasm, "I'd love to come."

"She thinks I can't cook," Mrs. Truscott told Rog with no rancor.

Nan laughed. "You can't. Even Aunt Char said so, and she never said mean things about anyone."

Mrs. Truscott lifted a tree ornament from its box and spun it by its gold thread hanger.

Nan grabbed the ball. "Careful! When I give it back, I don't want it chipped."

Mrs. Truscott's eyes widened. "You're going to give it back?"

"It isn't mine."

"It's a gift."

Nan rolled her eyes and put the ball and all the other products of leavery under the counter. "What time for dinner?"

"Let's say six-thirty."

Nan kissed Mrs. Truscott's wrinkled cheek. "Fine. Both Ingrid and Tammy will be here to cover the store. I'll be up at six-thirty."

A young woman in those shin-length pants Rog found a mystery—they were neither shorts nor slacks, so what was the point?—and a royal blue shirt with Present Perfect in gold script over her heart slipped behind the counter.

"Good, Tammy. You're back. Right on time." Nan looked at Rog and swung an arm toward a door in the back. "We can talk in my office."

He followed her as she came out from behind her counter and walked across the rear of the store, glad he was finally going to get her undivided attention. He practically walked up her heels when she stopped suddenly.

"Oh, no! A Royal Doulton Toby mug." She picked up a large china cup that bore a remarkable likeness to Winston Churchill's bulldog face, a ceramic cigar jutting from his mouth.

"Another leavery?"

Nan nodded, her shoulders slumped.

"Valuable?"

"Probably. I'd have to look it up."

"Char wouldn't stock something like that." Mrs. Truscott had come over to investigate what they were looking at. "Too masculine."

Nan ran a hand across her forehead as if rubbing at a headache. She turned to Rog, her expression pleading. "Fix it! Please!"

Rog's heart tripped, and he wanted nothing more than to fix it for her. *Lori,* he reminded himself. *Lori, Lori, Lori.* "I can check the database, see if any of these items was stolen."

"Yes!" Nan looked so relieved that Rog didn't have the heart to tell her he expected to find nothing.

"Very fine thinking," Mrs. Truscott said. "I can see why you're one of Seaside's finest."

Rog raised an eyebrow at her, and Mrs. Truscott grinned. He couldn't help but grin back. He liked the feisty old lady.

"And while I have your attention, young man," she continued, "I'd like to invite you to dinner this evening too."

Taken by surprise, Rog managed a very articulate, "Uh."

Mrs. Truscott beamed. "Wonderful! You can pick Nan up."

"Aunt Bunny!" Nan hissed, her face turning a charming pink.

"Push tush." Mrs. Truscott waved her protest away. "You need someone besides an old lady to talk to. I'm just helping you meet people your own age."

Rog looked at Nan and shrugged. Truth be told, a dinner he didn't microwave sounded wonderful, especially with Nan as a companion. *Lori, Lori, Lori.*

"Where do you live, Mrs. Truscott?" he asked.

She pointed vaguely down the boardwalk. "Nan knows."

"Mother!"

The loud voice made Nan and Mrs. Truscott jump. He watched as Nan's face took on a guilty look while Mrs. Truscott's went completely blank.

"I should have known you'd be here." A well-preserved woman of fifty or so halted in front of Mrs. Truscott. "Honestly, Mother."

The newcomer couldn't quite keep the pique out of her voice, and Rog knew that if he heard the barb, Mrs. Truscott certainly did, too.

"Hello, Alana," Nan said politely but without welcome. "The answer is still no."

Alana looked displeased. "What if I'm no longer asking when you finally decide to say yes?"

"I don't expect to ever say yes."

Alana sniffed, then turned her back to Nan, which angered Rog. Ridiculous he'd have that reaction. Still, he cleared his throat.

Alana seemed to notice him for the first time. She scowled at him, then at her mother. "What have you gotten yourself into now?"

There was no attempt to hide the pique this time.

Mrs. Truscott opened her mouth, but Nan spoke first. "He's here to see me."

"Huh." Alana made the one word sound as if Nan had just fulfilled every bad expectation she'd ever had.

Again Rog felt his hackles rise. How did someone as cheery and personable as Mrs. Truscott have a daughter as graceless as Alana?

"Come on, Mother. We have an appointment, and you need to change." She took Mrs. Truscott by the elbow and turned her toward the front of the store. Mrs. Truscott went without protest.

Rog glanced at Nan, who was watching the mother and daughter with a distressed expression.

Just before they left the store, Mrs. Truscott pulled Alana to a halt.

"Come on, Mother." Alana's voice was abrupt and condescending. "You don't want to be late."

"I don't even want to go."

Rog had to smile at the touch of rebellion.

"Of course you do," Alana said with absolute certainty.

Mrs. Truscott angled her body so she faced Nan and Rog. The twinkle returned to her eyes, and she gave them a sly wink.

"Six-thirty," she mouthed.

CHAPTER THREE

Nan spun on her heel and walked to her office, Officer Eastman following.

"Is she always like that?" he asked.

"Unfortunately, yes. After Aunt Bunny's husband died about a year ago, Alana seems to have decided her mom's not capable of caring for herself."

"Is she?"

Nan frowned as she walked behind Aunt Char's big desk. "Of course! She's more than capable. She's sharp as can be."

"How old is she?"

"Seventy-five."

He sank into the old padded folding chair across from the desk. "Not that old these days. My grandparents are all in their late seventies, and they're hardly ever home. They love to cruise."

"The way Alana tries to control Aunt Bunny, you'd think she had money."

"She doesn't?"

"Wait 'til you see her apartment." Nan grinned and gave a mock shudder.

"What did her husband do for work?"

Nan shook her head. "I don't know. I never met him. I know Aunt Bunny because she was Aunt Char's best friend, but we're not really related. The aunt is a courtesy title, but she's decided she takes it seriously. She's taken me under her wing since I moved here last month, taking me up and down the boardwalk and introducing me to people. She's a one-woman support system, an expert encourager."

Officer Eastman held his pen over his tablet. "If you're new to Seaside, then the list of possible leavers can't be all that long."

"I've met several people, but I don't really know anyone except Aunt Bunny, and I wouldn't say I know her well. I know she's a widow, her husband was Joe, and her daughter"—she motioned toward the front door—"you've met. Grouchy Alana. Aunt Bunny's nice, she loves the Lord, and she can't cook. But that's about all I know. And with the season ready to start, the shopkeepers along the boardwalk are all too busy for socializing. And I'm too busy to have much time for anything but church."

He studied her thoughtfully. "This has nothing to do with anything but my curiosity, but where do you go?"

"Seaside Chapel."

He grinned. "Me too."

She smiled back. "It's where Aunt Char went, so it's where I've gone the past few weeks. I like it."

He nodded. "So how'd you end up in Seaside? And where did you come from?"

"I've lived in New York City for the past six years. I worked at *Pizzazz*." She saw his blank expression. "It's a women's magazine. I've been here in Seaside a little over a month."

"New York publishing to a boardwalk gift shop. That's quite a career change."

She told herself she wasn't offended that he sounded as if he thought she'd been fired and landed here by default. He wasn't the only one who viewed Present Perfect as a comedown. "You have no idea how excited I am to have this shop. My great-aunt left it to me."

She ran a hand over Aunt Char's desk, crowded with laptop, printer, catalogues, and stacks of papers she hadn't had time to look at yet. Boxes to be opened lined one wall, and a small bathroom in the corner held a For Staff Only sign. "I think I'm going to like being in retail, though at the moment, I'll admit I'm a bit overwhelmed." She shrugged. "Okay. A lot overwhelmed."

Not that anyone seemed to believe her about liking retail, especially her mother. After the reading of Aunt Char's will, Mom had looked at her as they stood on the sidewalk outside the lawyer's office. "Nan. Dear."

When her mother said *Nan dear* like it was two separate sentences, Nan knew something had displeased her. But she couldn't be in trouble with Mom. She hadn't done anything yet, though she knew she was going to. Aunt Char had posthumously answered her prayers.

"Nan. Dear," Mom repeated. "I know just the realtor to handle the sale of that boardwalk shop for you." Mom said *boardwalk shop* as if uttering dirty words. "With the proceeds, you can get a nicer apartment in New York. We'll keep Aunt Char's Vero Beach house for wonderful winter vacations, though why Char left it to you is beyond me."

"She liked me?" Nan suggested. A business in New Jersey and a residence in Florida.

"Well, she liked me too." Mom sounded annoyed. Sure, Mom and Dad had gotten money and some jewelry, but Nan had gotten the bulk of the estate.

Nan hugged herself. She was an heiress! An heiress whose prayers had been answered!

"I'm not selling Present Perfect, Mom." It was a wild and perhaps foolish decision, but something in her knew Present Perfect was her calling. For the first time in a long time, she felt excited about the possibilities. "I'm not selling."

"Nan. Dear." The pause between the two words was extra long. "You can't keep the shop with a job as demanding as yours."

"You're right." The very thought of handing in her resignation made her heart leap with delight. She and publishing were not a good match. She hadn't felt either job satisfaction or inner peace for some time, and Aunt Char had given her the way out.

"I love you, Aunt Char!" Nan spun in a circle on the sidewalk while her mother looked acutely uncomfortable at the inelegant display of emotion. Nan would have thrown her arms around Aunt Char's neck and given her a big kiss on the cheek if she could have.

"Nan. Dear. Please. Show some decorum."

For once, Nan was too happy to be bothered. "Oh, Mom, this is my chance!"

"*Pizzazz* is your chance. Why, young women all over the country would give anything for your opportunity."

Mom was probably right, but that didn't change Nan's mind. Her job meant way more to her mother than it did to her.

"My daughter's the editor at *Pizzazz*, you know," she loved to say, as if Nan ran the show. That she was really a lowly assistant didn't faze her mother. She worked at a prestigious women's magazine, one that featured celebrities and set style, and Mom took full advantage of the bragging rights.

"So you'll just leave New York? Leave the magazine? For the boardwalk?"

The scorn and disbelief made Nan cringe, but she stood firm. How often did a person get an inheritance that allowed for a real life change? Practically never, that was how often.

"I could kill Aunt Char for this," Mom said. "If she weren't already dead."

So here Nan was, in Seaside, New Jersey, taking over Present Perfect. Between the excitement and terror that gripped her, she wondered if she'd ever take a full breath again.

She looked at Officer Eastman. "When Aunt Char left me the store, I jumped at the chance to try something different."

"Won't this be seasonal?"

"I haven't figured that part out yet," she said. "But I needed to get out of the pressure cooker that was my job, a job I didn't enjoy. I'm young, single, and unencumbered. Now's the time to try." She shrugged. "October and closing for the winter are several months away." She didn't tell him that Aunt Char had not only left her Present Perfect but the apartment on the upper floor as well. She could live there all year round if she decided not to keep the Vero Beach condo.

"I want to take pictures of your found items," Officer Eastman said. "I can compare them with info in the databases. Not that I think I'll find anything. If someone stole these things, they wouldn't be leaving them lying around. They'd be fencing them."

"I know. That's what's so strange!"

"The footage from your surveillance cameras will be a big help."

She made an I'm-sorry face. She'd been expecting the request for the disks or tape or whatever was in the cameras. It was always one of the first things Kate asked for on *Castle*. "I have a guy coming next week to get the cameras up and working. The place was closed for several months due to Aunt Char's illness. Sea air, you know?"

Officer Eastman didn't look happy, but he just nodded. "Corrosion." His cell rang. He held up a finger and pulled the phone out. "Eastman."

In a few seconds he hung up. "Gotta go." He stood and turned toward the store.

"You can go out back here," Nan said. "Save you fighting the aisles."

He managed a quick smile through the frown that had appeared with the phone call. He paused halfway out the back door. "See you at 6:30. I'll call if I'm held up."

Nan felt herself color again. "You don't have to come. Aunt Bunny will understand."

"And miss a meal I didn't nuke myself? Not a chance."

The office seemed very empty when he was gone, so she walked the store, aisle by aisle, looking carefully for any unexpected items. She found none, a great relief. Maybe there would be no more, but she was afraid that was too much to hope for.

She smiled her brightest as she sold a Seaside plaque, paper napkins covered with fancy seashells that never littered the Seaside beaches, two watercolor prints of Adirondack chairs sitting on the beach, and a set of bright orange and hot pink plastic dishes she privately thought atrocious. When she went to the back room to meet the UPS man, Tammy took over the register.

As Nan opened boxes of new inventory, her mind wandered to the Wedgwood ornaments. There were twelve days of Christmas. Her culprit had left only three of the days. Did that mean nine more were to come?

At least she'd have an excuse to call Officer Eastman if they showed.

She scrunched her eyes as the thought flew past. No. No men, not even handsome ones with dark chocolate eyes and great smiles. She'd promised herself. Just good hard work and sea air. Tyler had taught her that no matter how good a man looked in person and on paper, he couldn't be relied on.

CHAPTER FOUR

Happy he got off his shift on time, Rog let himself into his place, the second floor of an old Victorian that had been converted into a two-bedroom apartment. Judging from the light and TV noise that met him, Mooch had made himself at home.

Rog walked into the living room and found the young man slouched on the sofa watching *Firefly*.

"How many times have you watched this show?" Rog asked.

Mooch turned and smiled. "Not enough." He clicked the screen black.

"When'd you get here?" Rog dropped into a chair—brown, serviceable, not uncomfortable. He glanced absently around his living room. The sofa wasn't too bad, even if the green and brown plaid was a bit eye-curdling. The lamps had obviously seen many years of service, and the shades were a dingy beige.

He shrugged. It all came with the place, didn't require anything of him, and didn't make his back hurt. What more could he ask of furniture?

"And more importantly, how'd you get in?" Rog gave his guest the evil eye.

Mooch grinned. "I have a key."

"You have a key?"

"You gave it to me."

"I did not." He had his moments, but he wouldn't forget that.

"You just didn't know." Mooch shifted to get more

comfortable. "Last time I was here, I saw a key lying on your bureau. I tried it in the front door, it worked, and voila!"

"You do know that's theft, and I'm a cop, right?"

"It wasn't theft." Mooch waved away the suggestion. "You were right there when I took it. If you'd objected, I'd have left it where it was."

Rog thought back to the time Mooch had come into his bedroom a month ago. Rog had been shining his shoes, eyes on the black leather, not the kid.

"Someday, Mooch, you're going to go too far."

"Yeah. That's what Lori tells me all the time."

At the mention of Lori, the image of the woman he'd met that day sprang to Rog's mind, and he blinked. Instead of the leggy redhead, a little dark-haired pixie who was dealing with an anti-thief materialized.

"By the way," Mooch said, "Lori says hi. She's getting married."

Rog waited for the bitterness or the anger or the hurt, but none came. "The doctor?"

"Yeah. He's a weasel."

Rog laughed. "He's probably a nice guy. Your sister isn't stupid enough to marry a rodent."

"She was stupid enough to let you go."

"I got the best in the break-up." Rog pulled himself from the chair. "I got you."

Mooch grinned. "And now you've got me for the whole summer."

Rog headed for the bedroom. "Now I've got to get me out of this uniform."

The TV clicked back on.

"And then we've got to talk. Set some guidelines."

Mooch groaned. "What is it with cops and rules?"

"Guidelines, not rules," Rog called as he locked away his gun. He could hear Mooch muttering, or maybe he was talking to the characters on TV, telling Nathan Fillion/Malcolm Reynolds his troubles. No, he was muttering. About guidelines.

When Rog was comfortable in cargo pants and a polo shirt,

he reclaimed the brown chair.

"Ok, kid, let's talk."

Mooch clicked off the TV again. "Do you think you could not call me kid? I'm eighteen."

Rog shrugged. "I'll think about it. Depends on how you do here. By the way, how'd you get here?"

"Lori and the weasel brought me. Then they ran."

It went without saying that they wanted to avoid what they thought would be an awkward meeting. He'd only seen Lori once since she'd dropped him, and it had been awkward, mostly because she acted as if they barely knew each other. He'd come to get Mooch for a ball game. Lori, obviously not aware he was coming, had answered the door. At the sight of him, she first looked horrified, then chilly.

Mooch galloped down the hall steps and came up behind her.

"Your former fiancé, Lori." He grinned at Rog. "See what you lost? He was a keeper."

Lori flushed, her eyes fixed over Rog's shoulder.

Mooch sailed happily out the door. "Come on, bro. We're going to have fun, unlike some people, who are staying home alone because they're losers!" He all but shouted the last because Lori shut the door as soon as he was through it.

After that she'd made certain she wasn't around any time Rog came for Mooch, who had somehow become like his little brother.

And now he was living here for the summer.

"No wine, no women, no whining, especially about church." Rog put on his stern cop face to prove to the kid he was serious. "You live with me, those are the rules."

"Where would I get the wine?" Mooch scratched his chin. "You don't drink. The town's dry. I don't have wheels. I don't have a choice."

"The town's dry as a bone. They just had a referendum last year, and the no liquor vote won by two-thirds."

"Bet that makes your job easier."

Rog nodded. "But there's still booze in town. It's just not

sold here."

"What's next? No women? I hope you just mean no women in the apartment, because I plan to explore the beautiful beaches full of beautiful babes enjoying the sun."

"You know what I expect, Mooch. You treat any girl you date with respect, or we will have trouble before summer's over. Which will be sooner than you think if you give me trouble."

Mooch held up a hand. "I got you. And I agree. I'm not a total jerk. And I won't whine with an H about church. I knew church came with living here for the summer. But I do have another thing to whine about. I'm bored."

"You've only been here a couple of hours!"

"So I get bored easily."

"Well, you're going to be more bored. I'm going out for a couple of hours."

Mooch frowned. "What about dinner?"

"I'm being fed."

"I bet she's cute."

She was, but he wasn't telling Mooch about Nan. "She's probably in her mid-seventies, if I'm any judge. A nice widow lady. But dinner is dinner."

"Yeah, it is. What do I do?"

"Hit the boardwalk and get pizza or something."

"You going to drop me off?"

"No, you're going to walk."

"Walk?"

"It's about five blocks."

"To the pizza place or to the boardwalk?"

"Pizza. You know you need to get a job, right?"

"I want a job. I want money."

"I may have a lead for you. I'll know more when I get home."

"The seventy-year-old lady has a job for me?" Disbelief laced his words.

"Just let me check things out more. I think you'll like it."

Mooch made an indistinct noise but followed Rog out of

the apartment. They walked together toward the boardwalk.

"You've got to be home by eleven, Mooch."

"Eleven? Are you kidding? I'm eighteen!"

"And I have to get up early to go to work. I need my sleep. If this is going to work, you need to cooperate." Unspoken was the knowledge that Rog didn't have to keep Mooch. "You don't have to go to bed if you don't want to, but you do have to be in. And you have to use earbuds for the TV. The apartment's not that big, and noise carries."

They walked up the ramp to the boardwalk. Two cute girls walked by, and Mooch peeled off. "Later, dude."

Rog shook his head. He wasn't sure what he'd gotten himself into by offering Mooch a place for the summer, but the kid needed someone, and he was it.

Present Perfect appeared in the distance, its royal blue sign looking as feminine as all the stuff inside. No wonder he'd not given it more than a passing glance before. He grinned. He had a very good reason to notice it now.

CHAPTER FIVE

Nan knelt before a box in the storeroom and pulled bubble wrap from ceramic angels destined to hang on the Christmas tree in her holiday corner. She studied the little figurines. While she liked most of Aunt Char's inventory, she wondered about these angels. To her eye, they were tacky and poorly executed. Suddenly the task of providing product for the store felt crushing. What did she know about what boardwalk shoppers liked?

"Aunt Char, I don't know if I can do this."

It was one thing to work here in the summers through college, to put items on display, stand behind the register and take people's money, even do some bookkeeping. But buying inventory? Assessing what people were willing to spend money for? So many small businesses failed. What if she didn't have Aunt Char's magic touch? What if she couldn't measure up to the trust given her?

She was struggling to become familiar with the items sitting on the shelves, and in a never-ending flood, new inventory was being delivered every day, things Aunt Char had ordered months ago but which had delayed delivery dates. How was she ever to learn it all? Even now, product could be walking out the front door every day and she'd never miss it.

The sweat that popped out on her forehead had nothing to do with the heat. She ran a hand down her face. *Oh, Lord, I'm never going to be able to do this!*

How she wished she heard Him answering, "You'll be fine, my child. I promise."

Her phone played her mother's ringtone. Nan sighed. Mom was the last person she wanted to talk to when feeling so fragile. She straightened her shoulders and made herself answer.

"Nan. Dear. How are you today?"

"Fine, Mom." Well, maybe not *fine* fine but definitely finer than she'd be if she were still slaving at *Pizzazz*.

"Good. You know how we worry about you down there."

Nan rolled her eyes. Mom made Seaside sound like the farthest tip of South America, not a mere couple of hours from home. "I love it down here, Mom."

"So you keep saying. What time can we expect you on the Fourth?"

July Fourth? "On July Fourth I'll be right here taking advantage of one of the season's biggest weekends."

During the silence following her comment, Nan realized what her mother was talking about. The Party.

"But Nan. Dear. It's our party."

One of her mother's two big events of the year. The other was her Christmas party.

"I'll be there at Christmas, Mom. I promise. But I can't come for the Fourth. I just can't."

"But you never had a problem attending when you were at *Pizzazz*."

"At *Pizzazz* I had holidays off. Here I have to work to take advantage of them."

"But it's your store. Hire someone to cover for you."

Sure, Mom. I'll snap my fingers, and someone will appear. Nan counted herself lucky to have Tammy and Ingrid to help her, and she needed at least one more person, preferably one who didn't mind lugging stock around. When high season kicked in the first week in July, it'd be all day, every day for her. There would be no dinners with Aunt Bunny and no parties at her parents' place until after Labor Day.

Nan slid from her knees to sit, pushing herself back against the side of her desk. She propped her elbow on one knee and slid her fingers through her hair. "Mom, I'm sorry; I can't possibly come."

"It's only for a day, two at the most." Hurt rang in her mother's voice, hurt and censure.

Nan didn't know what to say.

Mom's sniff carried clearly over the phone. "One would think you were fifteen, rebelling in this petty, thoughtless manner."

Nan's spine snapped straight. "Mom, I am not rebelling, and it's only a party."

An outraged gasp hit her ear.

"A lovely party," Nan added quickly. "A fantastic party." She made her voice gentle. "But Mom, it's only a party."

Another of those throbbing silences until, "But what will people think if you aren't here?"

Nan wanted to say that no one would care, but she held her tongue. The buzzer on the back door made her jump. Salvation!

"Mom, did you hear that? Someone's at the door. I've got to go." She clicked off and lurched to her feet. "Coming."

She opened the back door to the store to find Officer Eastman standing there in civilian clothes, khaki cargo pants and a deep brown knit shirt that matched his smiling eyes. He'd looked strong and authoritative in his uniform, but now he looked—she struggled for the word. Adorable came to mind, and she clamped down on the thought. He looked hungry for his non-microwaved dinner, that's what he looked, and she wasn't ready to go.

She caught a glimpse of herself in the mirror on the outside of the staff bathroom door. Lots of words came to mind. Disheveled. Dirty. Wrinkled. Pasty-faced. She automatically fluffed her hair.

"I lost track of the time. I'm a mess. I've got to freshen up." Which she probably wouldn't bother doing if she were going to dinner on her own. Aunt Bunny wouldn't care what she looked like.

As she hurried to the store, she noticed he didn't contradict her about being a mess. Ouch. "Tammy, you're in charge. I'll be back in an hour or two."

Tammy waved as she continued to write something for a customer. "No problem."

Nan hurried back to the office and found Rog filled the small space with testosterone just by standing there. She took a deep breath and pointed toward the back wall. "Steps."

He looked confused.

"My apartment. Steps." She slipped past him and started up the inside flight from the office to the apartment. "Come on."

He paused at the bottom. "You planning to paint?" He pointed at the paint cans and supplies bunched up against the back wall.

She stopped, one foot up a step from the other, and glared at the paint. "It was the plan."

"*Was* being the operative word?"

Nan sighed. "The bedroom needs painting badly, and I had great ideas when I first moved in. Then I started to understand the demands of Present Perfect. Maybe in the fall when I can breathe again. If the shade of pink in the bedroom doesn't drive me nuts first."

"At least most of the time you spend in your bedroom you have your eyes closed." His footsteps fell firm on the treads behind her. "Is there another entrance to your apartment?" It was clear from his tone that he thought there should be.

"A front door down on the boardwalk and a staircase, so you can enter the apartment without going through the store or office."

He made a little sound as if that satisfied him.

She led him into what had been Aunt Char's summer residence. Most of the furniture was still Aunt Char's—her own was in storage near her parents' place in Devon about twenty miles west of Philadelphia on the Main Line—and Nan felt she was coming for a visit every time she stepped through the door. That it all now belonged to her still made her blink in disbelief.

Decorated in shades of blue and white, the living room screamed beach house but with class, not kitsch. Original watercolors of beach scenes covered the walls, but the best feature of the room was a large picture window that looked out over the boardwalk, the beach, and the ocean. A pair of swivel chairs sat in front of the window, and Nan loved turning one so she could look out as she read her Bible and prayed each morning.

Mom had wanted to rearrange the room the day Nan had moved in, putting the sofa in front of the window.

"But that blocks the view," Nan protested.

"It balances the room." Mom had definite ideas about *feng shui.*

Nan chose not to argue. "Let's go down and see the store."

Mom's back straightened. "I have to go. It's getting late."

It was two o'clock. "Mom, come on."

Mom gripped her purse and headed down the front stairs to the boardwalk. "I just can't, Nan. I am so distressed. You're making such a terrible mistake."

Mom left, but the chairs stayed where Nan loved them.

Officer Eastman looked around and smiled. "Very nice place."

"Thanks. I love it. Another gift from Aunt Char."

"Too bad I don't have an Aunt Char. I'd work hard to be her favorite nephew."

Nan grabbed a bottle of water from the refrigerator and offered it to him. "Have a seat..." She skidded to a verbal stop. "Okay. What's your name? I can't call you Officer Eastman all night."

He grinned. "Rog. Roger. Rog Eastman."

"You don't meet many Rogers these days."

"I'm usually the only one. If someone calls, 'Rog,' I know they're calling me."

"Well, have a seat, one and only Rog. I won't be long. Oh, a black and white cat may slink out from wherever she's hiding. She was Aunt Char's and is still reeling from her disappearance. I'm encouraged, though. Last night, she sat in my lap for about ten seconds."

"I'll keep an eye out." Rog walked to the picture window.

"Wow, this is wonderful."

She stood beside him as they watched the waves break, foam frothing gently on the sand. "I almost wish there'd be a hurricane or a nor'easter, not one bad enough that we'd have to evacuate, but one where I could sit here and watch the waves crash."

"Invite me over." He grinned at her. "Though in a scenario like that, I'll probably be working. Bad storms are all hands on deck."

Nan's phone played, and she pulled it from her pocket. She sighed. "My mother. Excuse me a minute, okay?"

She stepped into her pink bedroom. Why another call so soon? The last thing she wanted was an argument or an extended discussion that would change nothing. Nor had she the time. She glanced at the clock by the bed. 6:30. Even if she and Rog left this moment, they'd be late.

"Mom, I told you I can't come."

"But Nan. Dear. Brandon Tully's coming expressly to meet you."

Nan made a face. Ever since the Tyler debacle, her mother had decided it was her responsibility to find Nan a suitable man. While she had found an amazing number of unattached men, none had been suitable as far as Nan was concerned. "Who's Brandon Tully?"

"He's Clarissa Manning's nephew, and he works on Wall Street. He's very handsome. Clarissa showed me his picture."

How nice for Brandon, though if he was such a catch, why was his aunt acting as his dating service? She pulled off her dirty clothes and tossed them in the hamper.

"You'll have to apologize to Brandon for me, I'm afraid. I can't come. He'll have to meet someone else." She grabbed a red top from a drawer and a pair of cropped pants from the closet and tossed them on the bed. She ran to the bathroom, flicked the phone to speaker, set it on the vanity, and scrubbed the sweat from her face.

"What are you doing?" Mom demanded. "I hear water running."

"I'm multi-tasking, talking to you and washing my face." She applied a sweep of mascara to her lashes and a quick slash of blush to her cheeks. If you lived at the shore, shouldn't you have a natural blush from the sun? But that would require you had time to be out in the sun. "Mom, I'm not interested in a guy right now."

"But Brandon—"

"Gotta go, Mom. Tell Brandon I'll see him at Christmas. Love you. Bye."

She hurried to the bedroom, tossed the shirt on and stuck her legs into the navy pants. She rushed back to the bathroom to comb her hair. She gave a quick squirt with spray in what was undoubtedly a vain attempt to keep some order to her long curly hair. The wind and humidity would have their way no matter what she tried. She shrugged. It was only Aunt Bunny.

"Well, hello, pretty kitty," came from the living room as she slid her feet in her sandals. Rog had met Queen Elizabeth, affectionately known as Lizzie.

Nan grinned. It wasn't only Aunt Bunny. She grabbed a bottle of her favorite scent and gave herself a spritz.

In the living room she found Lizzie purring as she pressed herself against Rog's leg. He bent and scratched her head. If Nan remembered correctly, it was the first time she'd heard the cat purr since she moved in. Nothing like a good-looking guy to make a girl forget she was in mourning.

Rog straightened and smiled. The approval in his gaze made Nan smile back. Lizzie shot her a slit-eyed look of displeasure for breaking up what was clearly a blossoming love match, at least on Lizzie's part.

Nan gave the cat a quick ear scratch. "Sorry, Liz."

The cat shook her head as if flicking away Nan's touch. With a sniff, she stalked regally to the bedroom and her spot on the right-hand bed pillow.

"I'm not her favorite person." Nan led Rog down the front steps. "She wants Aunt Char."

"The past few months had to have been hard on her. She'll

come around."

Nan's phone played Mom's ringtone again, and the hairs on the back of Nan's neck bristled. She pulled the phone out, aware she was looking at it with eyes of narrowed displeasure, not unlike the way Lizzie had just stared at her. She bent and set her phone on the third tread. "Remind me not to step on it when I come home."

She walked onto the boardwalk and pulled the door shut with a satisfying bang.

CHAPTER SIX

Rog swallowed a smile as the faint sound of the phone filtered through the door. Score one for Nan. She might look like a pixie, but she obviously had spine. And wisdom. Leaving the phone was better than saying something you might regret when pushed a bit too far.

"This way." Nan led him to the left, into the most crowded part of the boardwalk. Pizza places, hamburger joints, ice cream and saltwater taffy stores, miniature golf, and game arcades all vied for attention, their signs beckoning in the evening sun.

"I love this time of year." Nan looked out at the Atlantic, waves breaking gently against the light beige sand. "Long days. Lots of sunlight. Warm temps."

"Tourists," Rog said as he halted to let a pair of boys run across the boardwalk in front of him, intent on the Johnson's caramel popcorn stand. He usually avoided the boardwalk in the summer unless he was assigned patrol here. Off season, he loved it, especially those early morning jogs.

He automatically peered at a group of five teenage boys making too much noise and creating chaos as they weaved through the crowd, bumping into people unnecessarily. He turned to watch as they passed, expecting to see a wallet lifted or a hand dipped into a purse. He couldn't decide whether he was disappointed or relieved when he detected nothing but boorish high spirits.

Off duty, he reminded himself as he turned back toward Mrs. Truscott's, though a cop was never really off duty.

"Problem?" Nan looked over her shoulder at the boys.

"Not that I saw. Just bad manners and disrespect."

He and Nan walked for a bit in an easy silence, the worn boards somewhat warped beneath their feet. Here and there a recent board replacement screamed, "I'm new!" by its light color as it nestled among its weathered comrades. The music pier rose out of the sea on their right, all pink stucco resting on fat pilings driven deep into the sand, the only building on the ocean side of the boardwalk. A marquee advertised a local band slated to play Saturday night.

He pointed at the sign. "Do you like concerts?"

She looked. "I do."

"Want to go?" The words jumped from his lips without premeditation. He glanced at Nan, who looked as startled as he felt. *Lori, Lori, Lori.*

"I can't." She held out her hands, palms up in the classic *I'm-sorry* position. "Work. It's the weekend."

Larger crowds. More customers. Only days until July Fourth. He couldn't decide whether he was relieved or disappointed she'd declined.

She studied him a moment, then looked back at the marquee. She cleared her throat. "Ask me again come September, okay? If you still want to, that is."

He nodded and thought he probably would. After all, she wasn't rejecting him. It was all about timing. Then again, maybe he wouldn't.

Lori, Lori, Lori.

It was time to change the subject.

"Does anyone work for you besides Tammy?"

Nan nodded. "Just Ingrid. They're friends." She stopped and stared at him. "You suspect one of them?"

Rog stopped too and looked toward the sea as people flowed around them, the human river parting for a pair of rocks. He'd been thinking of Mooch and his need for a job, but he did need to check out Ingrid and Tammy. Not that he thought they were involved. And not that there was necessarily a crime being committed if they were. "Where would someone their age get those things?"

"Exactly," Nan said. They resumed walking. "College kids don't have fancy china and ceramics lying around. They have college loans. And if their mothers owned the leavery items, surely they'd notice the things were missing."

"You'd think." He couldn't imagine a girl packing for a summer away from home and including figurines and bugles, but what if there were a family home here? "Do either of their parents have a place in Seaside?"

"Nope. They both live in Kentucky in the same small town. It's a case of Tammy deciding it would be fun to work at the Jersey shore for the summer and Ingrid deciding to come, too. Neither had ever been to the ocean before. They showed up looking for a job the first week I was here. Ingrid had already found a job waiting tables for breakfast and lunch, so she only works late afternoons and evenings for me. Tammy works from opening through early evening or from two until closing, as she is today. They've been great. I'm lucky to have them."

"And there's no one else? Working for you, I mean." No one else to check out?

"No, though I need to hire someone else."

"How about your neighbors? Any of them the type to leave you treasures?"

"One side is a bakery that sells coffee and great sticky buns in the morning and typical boardwalk food the rest of the day. Ed's Eats."

"A Seaside landmark like Shriver's or Johnson's or Carrie's Cafe."

"Really? I didn't know. Anyway, I don't see my leavery items coming from there. The

other side is Surfside, which sells T-shirts, beach patrol sweatshirts, sunglasses, beach towels—you know the kind of stuff."

Rog nodded. He had a sweatshirt and a pair of swimming trunks from Surfside. Big Mike owned the place and rarely moved from behind his cash register. He definitely didn't have

Wedgwood in his life. Disposable dishes with a fast food logo on them were his style.

Nan's case was fascinating, one of a kind, but it wasn't a real crime unless it turned out the items were stolen—which he thought unlikely. What thief gave away his swag? "I'll stop in tomorrow to check on things, Lori."

Nan nodded. "Thanks."

He smiled at her. She was so cute.

"So, who's Lori?" she asked.

His step hitched. "What?"

"Lori. Who is she? You called me by her name."

"I didn't." Even he wasn't that stupid.

She laughed. "Did so."

He replayed the conversation in his mind and heard himself say Lori. He sighed. All that reminding himself about Lori as a talisman against Nan had backfired big time.

"Let me guess." Nan grinned at him. "An ex, either wife or girlfriend."

He gave a little head tilt of acknowledgement.

"Girl or wife?"

"Girl. In my family, she's the name that shall not be mentioned."

"In my family, the name that shall not be mentioned is Tyler."

Tyler. Now there was the guy who was stupid, letting this pixie get away. "Does everyone have someone who was a huge mistake?"

"Probably. If they're older than sixteen. Do you miss her?"

"Nosy little thing, aren't you?" But he smiled down at her, so she'd know he didn't mind the question.

She turned a faint pink. "How do you know things if you don't ask?"

"Do you miss him? Tyler?"

"I did at first. Then I was furious at myself for hanging around so long, waiting for him to move off square one." She gave a little snort. "Well, he finally moved, right into someone else's arms."

"Ouch."

"Tall with legs, lots of legs, yards of legs." She looked down at her own short appendages.

Rog grinned as he pictured a tall woman with lots of legs, sort of a human octopus without the suckers.

She shrugged. "I'm over him. In fact, I'm glad it didn't work out. He isn't a bad guy, just bad for me."

He nodded. That was Lori to a T. Not a bad person, just bad for him.

"So back to my question." Nan turned those wonderful hazel eyes on him. "Do you miss her?"

"I don't. She rarely crosses my mind anymore." Unless he was using her as a warning to himself against cute brunettes.

"If you say so."

He heard the doubt, understandable since he'd called her Lori. "We broke up a while ago. Well, she broke up with me. Didn't want to be a cop's wife. When we started going together, she thought I was going to be a lawyer. I was in law school. But instead of taking the bar, I went to the Police Academy."

"Ah. From hourly billing to hourly danger."

He laughed. "Seaside isn't exactly New York or Philadelphia."

"But we've got leavery!"

"We do. We'll catch the villain when the security cameras are functioning again."

"I'm counting on you."

"Then I'd better succeed."

They walked a bit in companionable silence before he asked, "If Tyler's the name that shall not be mentioned, who's Brandon?"

She made a face. "You heard."

"It's a pretty small apartment."

She sighed. "He's some guy Mom wants me to meet. He's the nephew of one of her friends. He's part of her campaign to save me from the life of a retailer."

"What does she want you to be instead?"

"The editor of *Pizzazz*."

"Of course. But you like selling stuff?"

"I love it. I know it's corny, but I feel like I'm giving gifts to people, pretty things that they can use and that make them happy."

He narrowed his eyes as he thought about that.

"What? You think I'm nuts too?"

"Not at all. I was thinking about the giving of gifts after I left you earlier, especially the part about a purpose in giving. Working retail gives you a purpose in your 'giving.'" He put the word in air quotes.

"Purpose equals making a living. I hope." She pushed her hair out of her face, and the wind immediately blew it back.

"And making people happy. You just said."

"I did."

"What if someone is giving you gifts because he or she wants to make you happy?"

"He thinks he's giving me happiness?" She shook her head. "What he's giving me is a headache."

"You don't think it's possible the leavery is meant to be kind? Grace-gifts and all that?"

It was her turn to be thoughtful. "But it's like whoever is doing this is doing only half the process of giving."

"What do you mean?"

"I'm getting these—okay, we'll call them grace-gifts for the sake of your argument—but I can't do anything with them. Presents are supposed to be free to the receiver, right? Grace is. Real grace. God's grace. These presents have price tags attached as surely as if they said their actual retail value. And the tags read responsibility and inconvenience and frustration."

"So you're saying the giver is out to get you? To upset you?"

"Am I saying that? I don't know."

"Is there someone who would like to make you upset? Tyler, maybe? Tyler's new girl?"

"Tyler's wife, and I'm the least of their concerns. They're too busy living happily ever after."

"Anyone else?"

She looked genuinely distressed. "Why would someone want to upset me? I'm nice to everyone. Even my mother. Most of the time."

He laughed. He couldn't remember the last time he'd enjoyed such verbal jousting with a girl. "You feel guilty, don't you, about leaving the phone on the step and unanswered."

"My mother and my guilt are complex topics I don't wish to discuss. Why ruin the evening? We were talking gifts. Aren't they supposed to be useful and used? Something the receiver will enjoy?"

Rog shrugged, willing to go back to talking about gifts. Just because he was interested in her and everything about her didn't mean he should expect her to feel the same. As a cop, he might be able to ask the most personal of questions and expect an answer, but as a guy who thought a girl was cute, there were boundaries. He had to earn her trust if those boundaries were to fall, and they had to fall to Rog Eastman, not Officer Eastman. "The giver usually thinks the gift is good, even if the receiver doesn't. Hence re-gifting."

She stopped again, hands on hips as she glared at him. "Are you saying I'm supposed to re-gift that stuff? Just accept it and use it somehow?"

"Well, no." He stopped beside her. "Maybe. But I don't think the issue is worth all the angst you're giving it. It's interesting, fascinating in fact, but on a scale of one to ten..."

She started to walk in quick, frustrated strides. "Easy for you to say. You don't have those things showing up at the police station."

He laid a hand on her shoulder. "I'm not discounting your distress. I'm just trying to put it in perspective. When I got that call and had to leave your place? It was about a little girl disappearing on the beach. Anguished parents. A big ocean. Lots of unknown people, one of whom could be a pervert."

Nan took a deep breath, her hands raised. "You're right. Nobody's hurting me. I'm being given pretty things. It's not terrible. Ridiculous and weird, but not terrible. Did they find

41

her?"

"They did. She'd wandered down the beach a few blocks. A kind lady saw her looking lost and took her to a lifeguard, who called the lifeguard captain, who returned her shortly after I got there. All's well that ends well."

Nan grinned up at him, eyes shining. "I'm so glad. That allows you to enjoy tonight without a black memory hanging over you."

Rog blinked. A sparkling grin like Nan's would make any man forget black memories and think, "Wow!"

Lori, Lori, Lori.

CHAPTER SEVEN

Nan watched the huge Ferris wheel turn at Buchanan's Buccaneer Bay on the Boardwalk. Not that anyone called the amusement park by its full name. Most people called it the Buc.

Music that was supposed to sound like a pirate's shanty blared through loudspeakers. A huge pirate ship with a flying Jolly Roger sat over the vast doorway to the amusement complex, cannons sticking out in every direction. In a series of loud booms, they fired one after the other, each one emitting smoke. A pair of teenage boys appeared on a gangplank, one with his hands tied in front, the other with a sword, making him walk.

"Die, you vermin, you!" shouted the PA system, the lips of the kid with the sword moving in sync with the words.

A scream rent the air as the captive fell to his death. The remaining pirate did a victory dance. The pirate shanty played again at full volume.

"Does that kid have to die all summer?" Rog shook his head in wonder. "Talk about being hard up for a job."

"Makes me think of the woman who rode the diving horse on Steel Pier in Atlantic City."

"I don't think this kid ends up in a pool of water."

"I wonder what he does end up in."

"Something soft," Rog said. "I hope."

"Let's go for a ride after dinner." Nan felt a rush of anticipation at the thought. "Maybe the Tidal Wave or the End of the World. That's my favorite." She glanced at Rog to see a look of horror on his face.

"That's the one where they take you way up and then drop you," he said. "Up, down, up down. Right?"

"Of course. You're falling off the end of the world." She laughed. "You're turning green!"

"I might as well confess and get it over with. I can't stand amusement rides. Inner ear issues. They all make me nauseated."

"Even the Flume—or as the Buc calls it, Ride the Tide? You only go down once."

He shook his head.

"The Ferris wheel? The merry-go-round?"

"If I take my Dramamine first—which I didn't tonight. Wasn't planning on riding."

"Poor guy." Nan meant it. She loved amusement rides.

"I know. Not very manly. As a teenager, I was the amusement park equivalent of a designated driver whenever my friends and I went to one. I held all the purses and sweaters while everyone else rode."

"You could have stayed home."

"And miss all the fun? Or I should say, and miss being mocked?"

They joined the people pouring into the Buc to get their thrills for the night. The cannons boomed, and the kid walked the plank once more. The victorious pirate raised his arms in victory, and the crowd cheered. The shanty rang out.

"Maybe you could ride Choo-Choo Chugger?" She pointed to the kiddie ride moving slowly around its track, little people pulling ropes that made the bells on their cars ring.

"It's a circle. Besides, I doubt I'd fit."

She eyed his long, lanky frame. "Convenient excuse." She started walking deeper into the park. "Come on."

When he hesitated, she pointed to the windows on the second floor of the building abutting the park. "That's where Aunt Bunny lives."

"Next to this chaos?"

"I know. I couldn't stand it either."

They came to a scuffed red door tucked in the side of the two-story stucco building. Nan rang the bell beside the door, then opened it.

"Aunt Bunny, it's us."

"Of course it is," came the answer. "Come on up."

"I wonder if Alana's here," Nan muttered as she climbed the stairs.

The cannons boomed, the pirate walked the plank, and the shanty began.

"I can't decide what's worse, the cannons or the "Die, you vermin, you!" Rog did a fine imitation of the pirate. "The music is beyond grating."

"That was very good!" Aunt Bunny appeared at the top of the stairs. She'd changed her pink top for a red T-shirt that read Seaside Beach Patrol and had a large life preserver plastered across the back. She'd turned in her Reeboks for red flip-flops decorated with great red plastic flowers over the toes. "Do it again." At Rog's blank look, she said, "The 'die, you vermin' thing."

He stopped three steps from the top, struck a pose, and barked, "Die, you vermin, you!"

Aunt Bunny backed up, grinning widely. "They should have gotten you to make the recording."

"Would I have gotten residuals?"

"Don't suggest that to the kid who did make it."

The cannons fired, slightly muted by the closed windows and the hum of the air conditioner in the window facing the ocean.

"They had a hard time coming up with what the pirate should say." She got a sly gleam in her eye. "The language the real guys probably used isn't exactly family friendly."

The shanty played in the background.

"Does it play all day?" Nan asked.

Aunt Bunny walked to the side window and peered down at the controlled chaos next door. "No. The Buc closes at eleven every night and doesn't open until eleven in the morning."

Half the day quiet. "At least you can sleep."

"I miss the noise when it's gone," she said. "Now come to the table. Dinner's ready."

She led them through the living room with its Salvation Army castoffs and old fashioned TV to the eating area. Three places waited, inexpensive flatware flanking floral plastic plates resting on place mats like the beach scene mats Nan sold at Present Perfect. Sherbet-colored napkins and plastic tumblers also from Present Perfect matched the colors of the artificial lilacs and cyclamen that made up the centerpiece.

Three settings. Nan tried not to look too pleased. "Alana's not joining us?"

"Push tush, of course not. She can't stand it here." The cannons fired. "She says it's too noisy."

Nan laughed. "I can't imagine why."

Aunt Bunny grinned as she turned to a kitchen area the size of a small bedroom closet and pulled a metal bowl filled with ice cubes from the little refrigerator's freezer.

"Let me," Nan said, taking the bowl of cubes.

While she put ice in the glasses, Aunt Bunny pulled three shrimp cocktails from the refrigerator.

"Sit, young man," she instructed Rog. "Do you want sweetened or unsweetened iced tea?"

"Sweetened," Rog said as he sank into a chair that wobbled slightly beneath him.

"Careful." Aunt Bunny poured him a glass of tea. "This furniture is not the best."

But the dinner was. A delicious chopped salad followed the shrimp, and the entrée was breaded baked flounder—"I'm not allowed to have it fried anymore," Aunt Bunny announced as she served it—with garlic mashed potatoes and asparagus.

Rog scraped the last crumb from his plate and looked at Aunt Bunny appreciatively. "This was a delicious meal."

"Push posh," Aunt Bunny said. "It was nothing. All I had to do was tip the delivery boy."

"Then you have good taste in take-out."

Aunt Bunny laughed. "Make that one of the questions you ask any girls you date. Do you cook?"

"What if they say no?"

"Then ask yourself how much you like pizza. You'll be eating a lot of it."

Rog choked on his iced tea.

"You don't think I ordered like this every day for Joe, do you? But he never complained." Her voice grew soft and her eyes sad. Then she gave a little head shake and forced a smile.

Nan stood and gathered the empty plates. "Well, thank you for doing it for us, Aunt Bunny. It was wonderful. Does Alana cook?"

"Oh my, yes. Gourmet. Undoubtedly a reaction to my lack of skills."

For a moment, the only noise besides the distant shanty was Nan scraping the dishes.

Aunt Bunny gave a large sigh. "Alana wants me to go to a retirement home."

Nan looked up, startled. "Is that why she's been bothering you?"

"One of the reasons."

Nan kept herself from looking around the small apartment with its limited space and worn furniture. "Are you going to go?"

"If I do, it won't be because Alana is pushing me." Aunt Bunny stalked to the refrigerator and pulled the freezer open. She brought out vanilla ice cream and began scooping it onto slices of chocolate decadence cake. "I can make my own choices."

"And Alana thinks you can't?"

"She's decided that since Joe died, I am frail and incompetent." Bunny snorted her disgust. "Just because her friend Tessa moved her widowed mother from her home in Kansas to a retirement place in New Jersey three months after she was widowed, Alana thinks she should be making choices like that for me."

Rog poured himself another glass of iced tea from the pitcher on the table. "My mother's parents went to a retirement community last year, one of those where you start in a cottage and have care until you die. They love it."

"But I bet they chose to go. I bet no one forced them."

Rog nodded. "True."

"I went to visit Tessa's mother," Bunny said. "Talk about depressing. The poor woman is still grieving her husband of 52 years, and now she's also lost all her friends and everything familiar because her daughter pushed and pushed when she was vulnerable. They sold her house right out from under her. I know it's not criminal by your definition," she said to Rog, "but it's still wrong, wrong. What time is it?"

Nan looked at her watch. "Almost seven thirty."

Aunt Bunny nodded. "Good. Time for the damsel in distress." She hurried to the window overlooking the Buc. "Come on. You've got to see this. It's new this year."

Nan exchanged a look with Rog, who got to his feet.

"Hurry. You'll miss it." Bunny waved her hand to make them move faster.

Nan stood beside Aunt Bunny while Rog looked over their shoulders.

The cannons fired.

The pirate walked into view high above the heads of the crowd gathered below.

A young woman in an old-fashioned long dress was brought forward by another pirate, her hands tied before her.

"Tell me where the treasure is or you die," boomed the PA system.

"Never," the girl said bravely. "You are too evil."

"Then you walk the plank." He prodded her forward with his sword.

She walked bravely onto the plank.

As she stood on the very edge, the hero swooped in on a rope and dropped beside the pirate. With one strong thrust of his sword, he ran the villain through, pushing him over the side of the ship. The second pirate ran off in fear.

The girl raced off the plank. She threw her arms, which had come conveniently untied, about the hero's neck. The crowd cheered as they kissed and ran off together.

Bunny sighed. "Don't you love it?"

"How often?" Rog asked.

"Every fifteen minutes. That makes it special."

"Aunt Bunny, you're a romantic," Nan said as they returned to the table for their cake.

"Of course. I was married to Joe, wasn't I?"

In short order, dessert was eaten and the dishes were washed and put away. Nan started to think about the need to get back to the store. She was only confident about leaving Tammy in charge for an hour or so, even with Ingrid as her backup. Any longer made Nan twitchy.

"Time to go ride the Ferris wheel." Aunt Bunny started for the steps. "Come on. It's my favorite ride anywhere, but the one here is extra wonderful!"

"Rats, Aunt Bunny. I have to get back."

Bunny looked crestfallen. "Just one ride? Please?"

Nan gave in, not that she was fighting hard. "What's five more minutes? I love the Ferris wheel too."

Aunt Bunny laughed and headed down the stairs at a good clip, pulling on a ratty gray sweater as she went.

"You don't have to ride, Rog," Nan said softly.

"After that dinner? Sure I do. A little nausea's a fair price."

"Not if you lose said dinner."

"There is that."

Aunt Bunny's voice echoed up the stairwell. "You'll love it, Rog. I know you will. Rocking up at the top with Nan—the best."

Rog turned a pale green at the thought. "Sounds like great fun," he managed, and Nan had to laugh.

CHAPTER EIGHT

Nan inhaled the smell of popcorn, cotton candy, and hot dogs as they walked into the chaos of the Buc. Aunt Bunny waved at the kid manning the hot dog concession as they passed.

"How's it going tonight, Tim?"

"Pretty good, Mrs. T."

"Keep up the good work."

Tim grinned.

"Ramon, how's tricks?" Aunt Bunny called to the man in the ticket booth.

He stuck up his thumb. "Busy night, Mrs. T."

At the foot of the Ferris wheel, Aunt Bunny spoke to a young man in a black T-shirt. "Give my friends a nice long ride, Pierce."

"Aren't you coming with us, Mrs. Truscott?" Rog asked.

"Not this time. This is a ride for the two of you young people."

With a monosyllabic grunt, Pierce opened the bar across the seat and urged Nan in. Rog joined her with the expression of a French aristocrat going to the guillotine. The bar clicked, and the wheel began moving.

Nan looked down and waved at Aunt Bunny, who stood smiling up at them. "Wave to her, Rog."

He kept his eyes fixed straight ahead but managed to give his hand a weak little flip.

The car approached the top, and Nan looked out over the boardwalk with its noise and crowds. Then she looked farther to her left, over the beach to the ocean and up to a sky still a bright blue at—she glanced at her watch—seven-fifty. The beautiful golden light of evening made everything so lovely she felt tears. She was part of this wonderful town, this amazing boardwalk.

Oh, God, please tell Aunt Char I said thanks! Tell her I'll make her proud. I will. You'll see.

She settled back against the seat and took a deep breath. The Ferris wheel's movement stopped, and they sat at the very top, high above the world and its worries about paying bills, ordering appropriate inventory, and dealing with mysterious items. Rog sat rigidly beside her.

"This is where Aunt Bunny says we should rock," she teased.

He slid his eyes toward her. "If you do, I'll call it self-defense when they haul me in for murder."

She had to laugh even as she felt sorry for him. Poor man. He was just trying to make Aunt Bunny happy. She had to distract him from his distress.

"Tell me about Lori." It was the first thing that popped into her mind.

He turned his head slightly in her direction, looking as if he expected to fall out of the car with the movement. "What? Why?"

"I'm trying to take your mind off the ride."

"Um." He faced front again. "Will the descent be better with my eyes open or closed?"

Nan patted his shoulder as they started down. He closed his eyes and groaned softly.

When they neared the bottom, she waved at Pierce. "Let us off, please," she called. "I've got to get back to work." She promised herself she'd come back another time and take a long ride. A long, long ride.

When they exited, Rog only slightly wobbly, Bunny was waiting for them. "That was quick."

Rog opened his mouth to explain but swallowed quickly instead. It was the green cast to his face that had Nan speaking up.

"Work, Aunt Bunny. I've been away too long as it is."

"Well, I'll walk you out. Want a hot dog or some cotton candy?"

Rog made an *urp* sound, and Nan answered for them both again. "After that wonderful dinner? Maybe I'll be hungry again by morning, but not now."

Aunt Bunny looked pleased.

As they walked toward the bustle of the boardwalk, Aunt Bunny waved to many of the workers, calling them by name, and they smiled and waved back.

"You know everyone who works here," Nan said.

Aunt Bunny shrugged. "I probably don't know some of the new summer hires, but I know a lot. They come back summer after summer." There was pride in her voice. "They're like family to me."

And from what Nan could see, they treated her with more affection and respect than her own daughter. How sad was that?

Nan and Rog were more than a block from the Buc before the noise of the cannons faded.

"How can she stand living there?" Rog wondered.

"I've asked myself the same question," Nan said. "But she's lived there as long as I've known her."

"And how long's that?"

"Ten years. When I worked for Aunt Char while I was in college, Aunt Bunny was in that apartment even then. Who knows how long she and Joe lived there before I met her."

Rog glanced back. "All year round?"

"Good question. I don't know. I guess I always assumed not. It screams summer only to me, but I don't know where they live..." Nan caught herself. "Where *she* lives the rest of the year."

"Where did your aunt live off season?"

"She had a condo on the ocean in Vero Beach, Florida. She had a store there for several years, but she sold it some time ago."

"She was never married?"

"No. A career woman."

"She must have been successful to live on the ocean. Not an inexpensive setup."

"I never saw her Florida place, and now I own it." Nan shook her head. "Weird."

Rog studied her for a moment. "Will you move to Florida off season?"

"I don't think so. It doesn't interest me. Maybe if I were older or married, but one new life a year here in Seaside is enough for me. I think I'll sell that place to finish paying off college loans and give myself a little more of a nest egg until I see what Present Perfect does." Another of her plans that wouldn't make Mom happy.

"So you're here permanently?" Was that pleasure she heard in his voice?

She nodded. "Though I've never been here off season before."

"Slower pace but still plenty going on."

"I think a slower pace will suit me fine. I feel like I've jumped from one rat race to another with the move from *Pizzazz* to Present Perfect."

"Makes jobs like painting the bedroom a fond fantasy, doesn't it?"

"Maybe by January I'll get to it."

"How about I paint it for you?"

The question was so casual and so unexpected, she wasn't sure she'd heard right. She glanced at him, and he smiled at her.

"I wouldn't want a pink bedroom either." He gave a mock shudder.

She laughed. "I just bet you wouldn't. But, Rog, that's asking a lot of you."

"You didn't ask. I offered."

"You're serious?"

"Why not?"

She could think of several reasons—not his place, time lost, he hardly knew her—but she chose not to list them aloud.

"I could come tomorrow night after work and get started."

They stopped outside Present Perfect, and she studied his face. She told herself not to read anything personal into his offer. He was just being nice.

Still, she'd see him twice tomorrow, once as competent Officer Eastman when he came to photograph the leavery items, and once as Rog, the adorable guy who, she was afraid, could make Tyler a long-forgotten memory

"I feel it's an imposition—"

He held up a hand. "No imposition. I volunteered, remember?"

"True, but still."

"I happen to like to paint. I worked my way through college that way."

"Are you sure?"

"Nan." He sounded slightly exasperated. "I wouldn't have volunteered if I didn't mean it."

She still had trouble believing in his generosity. "I've got nothing against pink in general, you know. It's just that shade."

He nodded as if he understood.

Adorable didn't begin to cover it. "Then I'll cook dinner for you. It's the least I can do."

"Yes." He fist-pumped the air. "Two nights without microwaved stuff. Mission accomplished."

"It's 'Be kind one to another,' you know, not 'Finagle a meal from one another.'"

He grinned. "Maybe I can manage both."

No, *adorable* wasn't even close.

They walked into the store to find a line at the cash register. Tammy was ringing up people as fast as she could.

Nan felt a surge of pride and hope. If there were this many here in June, what would July and August be like?

"Nan," Tammy called. "We've been waiting for you." She jerked her thumb toward a woman in shorts and a Seaside T-shirt. "Marcy here wants to buy these, and I couldn't find a price."

CHAPTER NINE

Rog peeked over Nan's shoulder at the pair of tall silver candlesticks sitting on the counter. They were quite fancy and very shiny. Real silver, he'd guess, not plate, and clearly more leavery.

"They don't have a price tag." Marcy ran a finger over one as she smiled at Nan. "Aren't they lovely?"

Rog waited with interest for Nan's response. He watched her close her eyes for a moment, take a deep breath, and then smile at Marcy.

"I'm so sorry. I'm afraid they're not for sale. I apologize for the misunderstanding." Her face flamed with embarrassment.

"Not for sale?" Marcy squinted at her, not at all happy. "Look. I want them. I'm willing to pay for them. And I've already waited thirty minutes for you to get back from dinner. I've got a tired husband and three very unhappy little boys waiting outside, chomping to go to the Buc."

Nan looked pale, and Rog bet the fish and shrimp she'd eaten were starting a war in her stomach.

"I'm sorry," Nan said again. What else was there to say?

With a few choice words that Rog hoped the woman's sons didn't pick up on, Marcy stormed out of the store. He could see her gesticulating as she told her husband and three boys about her thwarted desire. The man looked back into the store, eyebrows raised. He said something to the woman and took a step, but she shook her head.

Don't make a scene. Don't make a scene. Rog wished he could send the message telepathically. *Just leave.*

With one last fulminating glare from Marcy, she and her family disappeared from view.

Nan grabbed the candlesticks and stalked to her office. Rog trailed her and found her sitting behind her desk, glaring at the latest leavery.

"They showed up while we were at dinner?" He closed the door, shutting out the store, the boardwalk chaos, and the muted sounds of the sea.

Nan put the candlesticks on the desk. "I didn't see them before we left." She leaned back in the chair. "Whoever this person is, he or she keeps putting me in such an awkward position."

He slid into the seat he'd filled that afternoon. "I thought for a minute Marcy was going to be a real problem."

"I wouldn't have blamed her." She looked at him with her eyes wide and begging. "Rog, you've got to solve this. You've got to."

He smiled. "Don't worry. We'll figure it all out."

He could see her relax at his words and fix that amazing smile on him. He took a deep breath. He could recite Lori's name all he wanted, but it wasn't going to help.

"I need to speak with Tammy," he said. "She may have seen something or someone. Would you ask her to come in?"

"Sure. Let me get her." Nan started for the door, then stopped. "Wait a minute. You're not on duty. You don't have to do this now."

He grinned, appreciating her concern. "It's not a problem."

Nan nodded and left the office. While he waited, Rog took the chair behind Nan's desk, the position of authority.

Tammy opened the door and peeked in. "Nan said you wanted to see me. Am I in trouble?"

Interesting question. "Not that I know of. Come on in and have a seat."

Tammy sank into the old chair and clasped her hands in her lap.

"You know about all the things that have been appearing in the store." Rog stated the obvious.

Tammy nodded. She looked at the candlesticks resting on the desk and at the other things sitting on the shelf. "I keep wondering why someone would just leave nice stuff like that. It doesn't make sense. I mean, you could sell them, you know?"

"Would you sell them?"

"If they were mine? Sure. Isn't that what most people would do?"

"Probably. Where would you sell them?"

She looked thoughtful. "eBay? Craigslist maybe. And there are pawn shops, right? That's where the bad guys sell stuff in the cop shows, though I don't know where any are."

"So selling makes sense to you?"

"It does. Everyone likes extra money." She glanced toward the shelf again. "It's nuts to just leave stuff."

"Have you seen anyone leaving these items?"

She shook her head. "I wish I had. I'm really curious."

"Did you leave the items?"

"What? Me?" She looked both appalled and offended at the suggestion. "You think it's me?"

"You're here every day, and it would be easy for you to do it."

"Yeah, but where would I get the stuff? That's the first step, right? You have to get the stuff before you leave it."

"Absolutely."

"So I think someone stole all those things." She waved at the shelf of leavery items. "But if you went to the trouble of stealing them, wouldn't you want money for them? Unless someone just likes the thrill of stealing or besting the cops or something." She laughed. "I guess there are people like that."

He nodded. "Where are you staying in town, Tammy?"

"I have a room in a big house over on Central. I have a roommate who goes to college with me. We're from the same town. She works here part-time."

"Ingrid."

"Right. You want to talk to her?"

"Eventually. Do either of you have access to lovely things like those left?" He gave her a flinty stare to see if she'd squirm.

She didn't.

"Not me. I came to town with two suitcases and a backpack. Ingrid too. I know 'cause we came together."

"How about where you're staying? Are there items like that lying around?"

"It's a summer rooming house, you know? Ingrid and I live on the third floor in a room. All we see of the place is the front porch and the staircase on the way up. But they rent out all the rooms, so I expect that, like ours, all they have in them is beds and bureaus."

"So you're saying I can cross you off the suspect list?"

She grinned at him. "Yes, you can. And Ingrid too."

"Okay. Have to check, you know."

"Eliminate all the potentials."

"That's right. By the way, that's a nice bracelet you're wearing." He indicated the gold and diamond tennis bracelet he was certain she hadn't been wearing earlier.

She held out her hand automatically, her expression that of a kid caught driving dad's car without permission. It took her a moment, but she managed to grin. "Isn't it lovely? It was inside a Wedgwood vase I found just after Nan and you left for dinner." She took it off and handed it to him. "I'm so glad you mentioned it. I put it on so it wouldn't get lost, but I forgot about it." She deepened her grin. "Or maybe I was just wishing it was mine."

He took the bracelet without comment.

"I think this is the first jewelry left," she said. "At least, it's the first I know about."

He leaned back in his chair and smiled at her. She could be telling the truth. Either way, she could be useful to him. "What I really want you to do is be on the lookout for anything or anyone who strikes you as strange or suspicious."

"You want me to be like a secret agent?"

He wouldn't have put it exactly that way, but the idea seemed to please her. "Interested in the job?"

She beamed at him. "I'm in."

He stood and reached over the desk to shake her hand.

"Thank you. I'll be checking in frequently, but if you see anything, let Nan know immediately, okay? And would you please tell Ingrid I'd like to see her?"

She left and he sat. She was an interesting kid. Lots of people got nervous when talking with the police, even when they were completely innocent. She seemed unfazed by his authority. He certainly didn't think she was involved in the leavery for the reason she'd stated. She'd sell the things if she took them. He looked at the bracelet lying on the desk top. On the other hand...

The door opened and Ingrid peered in. "You wanted to see me?"

"Come in and have a seat." He indicated the chair across from him.

She perched on the edge, clearly nervous. He went with an easy question to start.

"How did you end up in Seaside for the summer, Ingrid?"

"When Tammy suggested a summer by the ocean, I thought how neat that would be. So I came with her."

"And things are going well?"

She smiled. "I love it here. Did you know I'd never seen the ocean before? Now all I want to do is watch it. I don't like to get in it very far. I mean, you can't see what's there. What if something's lurking, waiting to get you?"

She looked so worried he had to comment. "In all my time here, nothing worse than a crab has gotten anyone."

She tucked her hair behind her ear, unconvinced. "There's always a first."

He nodded. "Have you seen anyone leaving things in the store?"

She shook her head. "And I've been looking. Do you think it's more than one person?"

Interesting thought. "Why do you ask that?"

She colored, embarrassed. "Well, if one person came in carrying all that stuff, wouldn't he have to have a big bag or something to carry it all in? And wouldn't you have to wrap the stuff up so it didn't break?"

His estimation of Ingrid rose. After he finished asking her questions, she left, and he sat a moment. A conscientious worrywart. That was Ingrid. Tammy, on the other hand, was a confident princess. He felt pretty certain that Tammy had been leader of the mean girls back in their high school in Kentucky, while Ingrid had lurked in the shadows, hoping not to be noticed. They were an unlikely pair to go adventuring together.

He walked into Present Perfect and found Nan patrolling the aisles, looking for leavery.

"Nothing more?" he asked.

"Tammy told you about the Wedgwood vase?"

"And the bracelet."

"What bracelet?"

"A tennis bracelet she found in the vase. It's lying on your desk."

She nodded. "Tammy's not involved in the leavery, right? Or Ingrid?"

"I'll check on them, but they're living together in one room for the summer. Sturdy furniture and clean sheets once a week. Hardly a place for a treasure trove."

Nan shook a snow globe with a lighthouse in it and watched the swirl of white. "You know what? I've decided someone thinks they're being nice. Grace-gifts like Aunt Bunny suggested. Maybe I should do what she says and just sell the stuff."

He held up a hand. "Wait until we get a full explanation of what's going on. We don't want to do anything until we know. I'll be over tomorrow morning to check on things."

She smiled up at him. "I'll be waiting."

He was whistling to himself as he left. It felt good to know someone was waiting, even if it was for Rog the Cop rather than Rog the Guy.

He made his way back to the Buc. He slipped through the throng to the red door and knocked several times. No response.

"You looking for Mrs. Truscott?" came a voice behind him.

Rog turned and saw a man of about fifty, hair feathered

with gray at the temples and a face deeply tanned. He wore a T-shirt with *Buc by the Bay* and a Jolly Roger on it. "I am."

"She's sitting in her favorite place, the bench across from the Buc. I just left her."

Rog nodded. "Thanks." He pushed his way through the crowd once again, feeling like a salmon swimming upstream against a rushing current.

Sure enough, Bunny Truscott sat facing the Buc with her back to the ocean, clearly enjoying people-watching. She looked up as Rog approached and smiled. "I wondered if you'd come calling."

"May I?" Rog indicated the space beside her.

"Please do. Looking up at you towering over me would give me a sore neck in no time."

Rog dropped down beside her, and they watched people in silence for a few minutes. When the damsel in distress had been rescued once again by the brave hero swinging in on the rope, he turned to Mrs. Truscott.

Before he could speak, she asked, "Are you going to arrest me? I've got a good lawyer, you know. He'll spring me in no time."

He couldn't tell if she was joking. "No arrests on the horizon. No crime's been committed."

"Make sure you remember that. How'd you know where to find me?"

"Some guy with graying hair and a Buc T-shirt told me where you were."

"Mike. I'll have to fire him."

Rog laughed. "He saw me knocking at your door and directed me here."

She nodded. "Nice man. He's doing a wonderful job running the place."

"As good as your husband?"

Mrs. Truscott gave a sad smile. "No one's as good as Joe."

"Being here without him's got to be difficult."

"You have no idea. Still, there's nowhere else I want to be."

They fell silent as the cannons roared and the pirate made

his prisoner walk the plank. Mooch would have loved being the pirate for the summer if he'd known of the job. It would be the perfect outlet for his dramatic tendencies, though he'd probably rewrite the script every time he came on stage.

When relative quiet fell, Rog looked at Mrs. Truscott. "I haven't been in Seaside for long, but I know the name Truscott and what it means. I checked. You are that Truscott."

Mrs. Truscott nodded. "Nan doesn't know who I am."

"No, she doesn't. She also doesn't know you're the leaver."

"You didn't tell her?"

"I needed to talk to you first, to be certain I was right. I also needed to check on the girls who work for Nan and make sure they weren't involved." He gave her his stern cop face. "And now I need to put a halt to something that's bothering Nan enough to call the police."

Mrs. Truscott squirmed. "It started by accident, you know. The first thing I left was the antique doll Char gave me when Alana was born. I planned to just hand it to Nan as I told her its story, but she wasn't there. I set it on the back counter leaning against the register. I left for one of my many meetings with the lawyers about estate planning. When I came back to explain, she was so excited about the doll. 'Look, Aunt Bunny! It's a mystery!' She expected someone to come in and claim it."

"And of course no one did. In fact, more things began appearing."

Mrs. Truscott took a deep breath. "I'm downsizing, getting ready to move. It's the worst job in the world." She gave a soundless huff of air as she stared into space. "I take that back. Mourning the deaths of those you love is the worst job. Then comes making decisions by yourself and learning to live alone. Then comes downsizing, just another indication of the losses that come with aging."

She turned to him. "How old are you?"

Rog blinked at the abrupt change of topic. "I'm thirty."

"You young people are in the collecting stage. You get an apartment and fill it with stuff. Then a condo or a small house. Then a bigger house. Stuff and kids and cars. Acquisitions.

Then one day you're old, and it's time to get rid of most of the stuff you've been collecting for years. The house you bought for your family becomes way too big. Ours was too big when it was just Joe and me, but at least he made noise. Now there's only space and silence."

She looked smaller and sadder than the feisty woman Rog had encountered earlier, and he ached for her. "You said the doll was a gift from Char. Are the other things you've left gifts from her too?"

"They are. I thought Nan would enjoy another connection with her aunt."

"She can't enjoy that connection if she doesn't know where the things are coming from and why."

She threw him a sardonic look. "You know, sometimes I hate logic."

Rog laughed as a spark of that feisty lady reappeared. "You have to stop, you know."

"Yeah, I know. I honestly didn't realize how upset she was until I saw you at the store this afternoon." An impish light appeared in her eyes. "It's been fun, sneaking stuff in myself and asking some of the kids at the Buc to be my emissaries."

"But no more, Mrs. Truscott. No more. Promise?" He intensified his cop glare.

"You're pushy. You know that?"

"I can be. I don't like seeing Nan upset."

Mrs. Truscott sat up straight and, smiling, patted his arm. "You like her."

Rog took a deep breath and stuck to his mission. "And you have to tell her it was you."

"Yeah, yeah, I know." She sounded incredibly grumpy.

"I want your word."

"I'll tell her. I promise."

"If you don't, I will."

She glared. "I said I'd tell her, and I always keep my word."

Her voice might be sharp with pique, but he was satisfied he'd gotten his point across. He stood and took a step away to break the tension that had built between them. He smiled. "I'll be checking to see you keep your word."

She narrowed her eyes at him. "You should be thanking me, you know. Without me, you wouldn't have met Nan, and you wouldn't have an excuse to keep seeing her."

He didn't let her see he agreed. "I'll see you at Present Perfect tomorrow."

As he walked away, he thought he heard her mutter, "Mr. Bossy Pants."

He grinned. Feisty was back.

CHAPTER TEN

Nan watched Rog Eastman's back as he walked away from Present Perfect.

"Nice looking guy," Tammy said, a dreamy look on her face.

"Too old for you," Nan said. *And just right for me.* She blinked, surprised and alarmed. No way. All she had to do was remember Ty.

"I'm nineteen," Tammy said defensively.

"And he must be in his late twenties, early thirties."

"So?"

Nan smiled. She wasn't getting into a discussion about the difference those ten years made, especially not with someone who worked for her.

"You just want him for yourself," Tammy said, eyes narrowed.

"Absolutely," Nan agreed. "I'm salivating here, dying for a man in my life."

Tammy heard the sarcasm, but her confused stare told Nan she didn't understand it. She couldn't imagine not going after someone like Rog. Of course, Tammy didn't know Nan's history either. She had no idea why Nan was leery of men, even those who seemed wonderful.

"Where is she?"

Nan spun to find Alana at her elbow. Oh, joy. The perfect ending to a long day.

Nan forced a smile. "You mean your mom?"

"Of course I mean my mother. Who else?"

Nan shrugged. "Well, I don't know. I saw her about"—she checked her watch—"about an hour and a half ago when she had Rog and me for dinner."

Alana looked aghast. "She had you at that apartment?"

Nan nodded. "We had a very nice time and a great meal."

Alana snorted. "Well, then she obviously didn't cook it."

Nan looked at Alana and thought of Shakespeare: *How sharper than a serpent's tooth it is to have a thankless child!*

"Oh, don't give me that look," Alana all but snarled. "She's not reliable. Surely you can see that."

Not reliable? Nan swallowed her anger at the slander. "I think your mom is delightful."

Alana's eyes snapped back. "That's because you don't have to deal with her."

"Why do you have to 'deal' with her? She's perfectly capable of taking care of herself."

"Please. You've seen that apartment."

"So it's not the best." If Alana didn't like where her mother lived, why didn't she help her get a better place? If the woman's clothes were any indication, she wasn't short of money.

"She needs to be in a place where she will be taken care of."

A chill swept Nan. "Does she want to go to such a place?"

"The child has become the parent." Alana looked as if she expected a presidential medal for nobility of purpose.

"Sometimes that is necessary," Nan agreed. "When there's illness or incompetency. But your mother is fine."

"She wanders around in shorts and tank tops like she's a teenager!"

"I don't think poor taste in clothes has anything to do with competency."

Alana looked her up and down. "I don't wonder you think so."

Nan frowned. She liked the outfit she was wearing, but her dislike of Alana soared. "I don't think Aunt Bunny wants to move. She's not ready for a change. You need to give her time."

Alana rolled her eyes.

Nan pressed her point. "Don't they say you shouldn't make any major changes for at least a year after a death? When and if she decides to go to a retirement community, she will choose wisely, I'm sure." If she could afford such a place.

"Little you know. Since my father died, she's been totally irresponsible with her money."

"Well, it is *her* money."

"She needs guidance, a firm hand."

Nan felt sure her mouth had just dropped open. "You want to take control of your mother's money?"

Alana had the grace to squirm. "I am saving her from herself."

Oh, please! "Did you ever stop to think that she's just grieving? She lost Joe and Aunt Char, her husband and her best friend, within months of each other. I think she's doing very well."

"Just how long have you known her?"

"Long enough." But Nan knew Alana had her there.

Alana flung out a carefully manicured hand. "My father took care of her completely. Without him, she hasn't the vaguest idea how to run her life."

"Alana, that's not true."

"It is. She wanders around in a daze day after day. She cries all the time."

"Of course she cries! Her life has been irrevocably changed. But she doesn't cry all the time, and there is no daze all the time. I love it when she drops in to see me. She's full of energy and enthusiasm. We had a great time with her this evening. After dinner, she took us to the Buc for a Ferris wheel ride."

"The Buc." The scorn in Alana's voice was scathing. "Awful place."

"I'm not surprised you think so."

Alana drew herself up. "I must remind you of one thing, Nan. She is my mother, and I will make choices about her that I feel are for her best." She spun and disappeared into the night.

Feeling distressed for Aunt Bunny, Nan walked to the register to close it out. She had a hard time getting her mind around someone like Alana. Even when her own mother was driving her crazy, she would never disrespect her by presuming to make choices for her.

Sure, there were situations when a power of attorney was necessary, or even when an adjudicated decision of incompetence was required, but certainly not in the case of Aunt Bunny. Nan grinned as she thought of the woman in her Bermuda shorts, white sneakers, and red bag, red hair iridescent in the sun. When she grew up, she wanted to be Aunt Bunny.

How had someone as wonderful as Aunt Bunny produced a daughter as demanding and critical as Alana?

She forced those thoughts from her mind as she reconciled receipts and cash. Since the bulk of sales were paid for by plastic these days, the job wasn't as time-consuming as it had been when she was in college, and the cash on hand wasn't nearly the amount Aunt Char dealt with in the past. Today, there was only a little over one hundred dollars above the amount she had opened the register with. She would have expected several hundred.

Still, it was comforting that there was an indoor staircase to the second floor, so she didn't have to carry the money outside at night. Not that she expected anyone to be lying in wait for her, but then she hadn't expected anyone to leave treasures for her, either.

When closing came, she waved Tammy and Ingrid goodbye and went upstairs. She collapsed in one of the chairs in front of the big window and looked out at a nearly-empty boardwalk and the blackness of the beach and ocean. She smiled. She was happy, deep down happy. Being in Seaside filled her with peace. She was tired and uncertain and afraid of her own incompetence, stalked by possible failure, but she was happy. Satisfied. Content. After years of doing what others expected of her, she finally felt good about her choices. *Her* choices.

She rested her head against the back of the chair. When she

felt herself sliding into sleep, she rose and wandered into the bedroom. She pulled back the covers on her bed and knew tonight was one of those times when lying down would be amazing, on a par with sliding into a warm scented bath on a cold winter's night.

She'd had no idea retail was so physically demanding. And time-consuming. And mentally draining. It hadn't been that way the summers she worked for Aunt Char. Of course, then she hadn't been in charge. Then she wasn't the one who was responsible for preserving the legacy and reputation of Present Perfect. Then all she had to do was put in her hours every day and go to the beach the rest of the time.

She smiled. *Thank you, Aunt Char, and thank You, God!*

A loud meow sounded from the bedroom door. Nan looked over to see Queen Elizabeth sitting there, eyes narrowed, tail twitching unhappily.

"What?" She indicated the bed. "Your pillow awaits."

Lizzie snorted—or was that a sneeze?—rose, and stalked out of the room. Nan turned toward the bathroom to brush her teeth when a loud meow and the clang of a metal bowl being pushed around filled the air.

Rats. She'd forgotten the cat's water. "Coming, Liz."

In the kitchen, Queen Elizabeth sat beside her empty overturned water bowl. The empty upright food bowl shone dully in the glow from the lights lining the boardwalk and streaming through the picture window. Nan grabbed the bag of dried food and poured a scoopful in the upright dish. She picked up the overturned one, rinsed it out, and filled it with fresh water.

"There you are, baby." She patted the cat on the head, or tried to. Queen Elizabeth ducked low to avoid her touch and started eating like she hadn't had food in days.

"I'm sorry I forgot, but it hasn't been that long," Nan told the cat, who paid no attention. "I'm not used to having a pet. Mother never let me have one. Allergies, she said."

The disinterested queen kept eating.

Wondering what else she'd forgotten, Nan started for the

bedroom again. She just wanted to lie down and sleep.

Her phone! It would still be sitting on the front steps where she'd left it when she and Rog went to Aunt Bunny's. They'd come in through the store, she'd come up the back stairs, and she hadn't given the phone a thought.

She rushed to the staircase and flipped on the light. The phone's bright pink case was visible even from the top of the stairs. She had laid the phone upside down, something she never did. Was that a subtle or not-so-subtle way to metaphorically silence her mother?

What a terrible daughter. It was one thing to ignore Mom during a dinner out—oh, boy, how to explain that without Mom being miffed that she'd go to Aunt Bunny's but not go home. What if she'd called because something was wrong? Maybe it had nothing to do with Brandon or the party. Maybe Dad was sick.

She grabbed the phone and stared at the screen. Four texts waited. As she climbed the stairs, she checked them. All from Mom, no surprise. She dropped into a swivel chair and started reading.

Really, Nanette. You need to pick up when I call. Ignoring me will not make my disappointment go away. Call me.

Are you so busy that you can't find a minute for your mother? Call me.

Brandon is such a sweet boy. You will love him. Call me.

See you soon. Call me.

Nan dropped her phone to her lap. How could she get her mother to understand? She began to type.

Mom, I cannot come home for the party. She started to write *sorry,* but she wasn't sorry, so she deleted it. *There's nothing to talk about. Fix Brandon up with someone else. Love you.*

As she thought about fielding more calls tomorrow, she stared at the ceiling, looking beyond the white plaster to wherever it was God lived.

Dear Lord, how do I cut the umbilical cord without doing damage to our relationship?

She hadn't realized it was still attached until recently. How dumb was that? Most people made sure the cord was cut during their teen years. Was Mom right when she said Nan was rebelling like some very late bloomer?

"No! This is not rebellion!"

Queen Elizabeth stared at her with wide, unblinking and beautiful green eyes.

"Sorry, Lizzie. Didn't mean to disturb you."

With a sniff, the queen went back to licking her paws and washing her face while Nan mused on the umbilical cord some more.

During her teen years, she hadn't had a rebellious spirit. Rebelling seemed foolish and illogical to her. She loved her parents. Giving them a hard time would make them sad and home uncomfortable. Who wanted such a home?

Sure, they had pushed her toward certain colleges, but she'd liked those institutions too. Maybe if they hadn't agreed on her final choice, she'd have felt the pull of the cord as she fought for her choice, but they agreed, and the cord hadn't pulled. They never said a word when she moved to New York, but she now realized that was because they were proud of her job, especially Mom. The old "my daughter's the editor at *Pizzazz*" thing.

And now they weren't proud. At least Mom wasn't. Mom who struggled to do and be what she thought was right and proper. Mom who felt she had to prove herself every day. Mom who lived with constant social anxiety. In Mom's eyes, being a sales clerk, which was how she now saw Nan, was a great fall from grace. How could she brag about that to her friends as a sign of her worth?

Which was funny, because Nan had much more authority and responsibility now than she ever had at the magazine.

With a sigh, Nan stood. "Come on, Liz. We're going to bed."

As usual, Liz ignored her. Nan bent and gave the cat a quick pat, starting at her head and flowing down her body and up her tail. Liz showed her amazing flexibility as vertebrae by vertebrae, she again ducked away from Nan's hand.

Nan sighed at the rejection and went to brush her teeth. When she exited the bathroom, the queen was curled on her pillow, her back toward Nan.

Weary as she was, once in bed and snuggled down, Nan couldn't sleep. The day played itself in her mind from the leavery items to the ride on the Ferris wheel to the confrontation with Alana. Front and center was Roger Eastman.

In the morning, he'd be here to take pictures, and in the evening, to paint. She felt herself smiling.

She looked around the bedroom, deeply shadowed with only a knife's edge of light seeping around the window shade. How had Aunt Char's usually-impeccable taste gone off the rails so thoroughly in here? She tried to picture the soft gray-green she'd chosen, but Rog, roller in hand and painter's cap on his dark hair, intruded. Did he even wear a painter's hat?

She scrunched her eyes and reminded herself of her man-rule. No men, not even adorable handsome ones with dark chocolate eyes and a great smile. She'd promised herself. There wasn't time for a man. There wasn't emotional energy for a man. Just good hard work and sea air.

Tyler, Tyler, Tyler. Remember Tyler.

"You're the best, Nan, the very best!" Ty would say as he hugged her. "I am so lucky to have you."

Five years he'd given her that line, two years in college and three after, and she'd loved it, just as she loved him. They got their jobs in New York to be near each other, spent their free time together, though there hadn't been as much time as she'd wanted. *Pizzazz* ate her life, and he studied for his MBA at Columbia. She'd been so proud of him.

"Is it finally time to get married?" she asked as they celebrated his graduation at their favorite restaurant. Since she knew being financially stable was important to him, she said, "With your degree, you'll get that promotion and raise. Between us, we can afford a really nice apartment even at Manhattan prices."

"Interesting idea," he said with a definite lack of

enthusiasm. "Sort of out of the blue, don't you think?"

After five years? She forced a laugh, because she couldn't deal with the idea that he was going to keep playing Mr. Hesitance.

One evening shortly after his promotion, they went for a walk in their favorite park.

"I've got some big news." He fairly glowed with excitement.

This was it. After his promotion came his proposal. Maybe he'd fall to his knee under that maple they loved because it turned so fiery in the fall and cast such wonderful shade this time of year. It was just around the bend in the path.

"I've met the girl of my dreams," he announced, "and I'm getting married."

Okay, she thought. Strange proposal, but at least he was ready to commit. "When do you want to do it?" She was thinking next summer, or maybe a destination wedding in the Caribbean in late spring.

"Jen says August, after summer school's over and before the new school year starts."

Nan froze. "Jen?"

He nodded, now looking vaguely guilty. "I met her through one of the guys in grad school. She teaches first grade."

Nan looked at him in horror. "You're marrying a girl named Jen." How could this be? He was supposed to be marrying her. For five years they'd talked about getting married. Or—shattering thought—had it been only her?

"Nan, you're my best friend." He reached for her hand. "Please be happy for me."

She whipped her hand behind her back. Be happy for him? Her heart was breaking, and he wanted her to be happy?

She realized she'd stopped walking. The maple tree was close, so close, just around the bend, and oh, so far.

She forced herself to take a deep breath. She had to leave and fast, or she'd wail her hurt. That would be more humiliation than she could bear.

She turned and hurried back the way they'd come, away from the maple, away from the man she loved, away from what

73

she'd thought was her future.

"Wait!" Tyler moved like he meant to follow her. "Wait, Nan. Don't be mad."

Mad? He thought she was mad like some junior high girl whose boyfriend took someone else to the dance? Was he so insensitive that he didn't get that her life had just imploded? He was an idiot, an insensitive idiot! A touch of anger gave her just enough iron to keep walking without her knees giving way.

"I want you to meet Jen," he called.

Nan spun. "What did you say?"

Tyler looked taken aback at her angry disbelief.

"You—" For once she wished she swore, so she could call him a name foul enough to match his actions. Instead she ran, almost bowling over a tall, leggy blonde. The woman jumped out of her way as she plowed on, hurt and humiliated to the depths of her soul. The peace and security she'd felt for so long because of Tyler was shattered.

"Nan," Tyler called.

She kept moving, but not before she heard the blonde say, "Let her go, Ty. I told you this was a bad idea."

CHAPTER ELEVEN

The first thing Nan did Tuesday morning was walk around Present Perfect looking for any new treasures. If she found anything, it would be breaking and entering, and the stakes would be raised. But how would someone have gotten in a locked store? She breathed a huge sigh of relief when nothing new appeared.

So when had the leavery items been left, and why hadn't anyone seen? Had breaking and entering already been committed in order to leave things? She didn't think so. There were no signs.

Were items missing from the store, things she couldn't identify because she didn't know her stock that well yet? Was the perpetrator doing a swap, sort of *I leave this and I take that?* But the things left were much more valuable than anything that might have been taken.

She stared at the useless camera in the corner above the register. Job One for the day: call the alarm company and get someone out here immediately.

She wandered next door to Ed's Eats and grabbed her coffee and sticky bun, then settled at her desk to wait until eight o'clock and an open office at the alarm company. She unlocked her top desk drawer to search for the company rep's card and froze. There, on elegant heavy cream stationery was her invitation to the dedication of a new wing at the local hospital, a formal occasion that began with a dinner at the yacht club over on the bay. With a frown, she ran her finger over the embossed-in-gold hospital logo on the envelope.

Nan groaned. Going to a formal dinner to honor an occasion that meant nothing to her was the last thing she wanted to do. She didn't know anyone going, she had no idea who she could take as her plus one, and she was too busy.

But the accompanying note, handwritten by the event chair—someone she'd never heard of—expressed how they hoped she would come in Aunt Char's place. Aunt Char had been on the committee that planned and oversaw the building of the new wing, the Buchanan Children's Place.

Charlotte Patterson was much loved and is much missed. Please come in her place as our honored guest.

Two tickets and an RSVP note had been enclosed. In a weak moment of sorrow over Aunt Char, Nan had sent a positive response.

She glared at the invitation, shoved it back where she found it, and slammed the drawer. She only had two days to figure a polite and believable way to back out.

She sighed. She wasn't that clever. She was doomed.

With a bite of sticky bun to give her energy, she studied the catalogues that threatened to eat her office. The sheer number of items available for stocking her shelves was overwhelming, and she hadn't even looked online or gone to a single gift show yet.

She rubbed her forehead as tension wrapped itself tight. The challenge wasn't only choosing which items to select for next year, though that was scary enough. After all, how did she know what vacationers would want next summer? But even more intimidating was deciding how much she should spend on inventory—and how much she could afford. She could threaten her solvency by purchasing the wrong stock or too much stock. And if people didn't buy what she'd chosen, bankruptcy loomed.

"How did you know how much you could afford, Aunt Char?"

When she looked at the amount of money involved if she purchased only the selected items from the catalogues, she swallowed hard. She wasn't used to dealing with figures like that. Sure, *Pizzazz* dealt in huge numbers in salaries and compensation, advertising revenues, production costs, and a multitude of other categories, but she wasn't responsible for those numbers being accurate forecasts of the magazine's health. That was up to other people. She kept an eye on petty cash for the office and rewrote advertising copy when she wasn't running errands.

Present Perfect's survival was her sole responsibility, and using her limited funds wisely was critical. There was some relief in knowing the Vero Beach condo was a cushion, but its sale would only provide so much help.

She rested her elbows on the desk and her forehead in her hands. She desperately wanted to succeed, but the fear of failing pressed down on her, threatening to crush her. She could hear her mother's voice. *Nan. Dear. I warned you.*

"Oh, Lord! Help! You said that if we lacked wisdom, You'd give it. I'm asking. I'm pleading! Please give me some wisdom, like You said You would."

She straightened, determined to create a workable budget for the store. She'd barely pressed pencil to paper when the buzzer on the back door sounded. Distraction had never been so welcome.

She flicked the lock and opened to Rog.

I'll be waiting. Her final words as he left last evening streaked through her mind as they had, say, a billion kazillion times since she'd said it, and the same flush warmed her.

Be cool, girl. There must be no more of that sounding overeager. Still, she grinned at him, happier than she expected to be at the sight of him, and not just because he saved her from the horror of budgeting.

He stood in the doorway, all official in uniform and sidearm. "What if I were a thief?"

She stepped back so he could enter. "Hello to you too. You're not a thief."

He remained in the doorway. "How did you know when you opened the door? Did you magically divine who was on the other side?"

Her smile dimmed. "It's eight in the morning. Who robs places at eight in the morning? Now, ten at night when I've got a full register, maybe, though with most transactions these days made with plastic, robbery isn't the for-profit profession it used to be."

He ignored what she thought was pretty good logic. "You need to ask people to identify themselves."

"Come on. Anyone can say he's the UPS guy."

"Peephole. Then you can see his brown uniform."

"Do cops always expect the worst?"

He shrugged. "It's what we see."

"Well, I'm an optimist."

He sighed and stepped inside. "I'll bring peephole stuff when I come to paint."

Nan blinked as she tried to figure out how she felt about that. On one hand, he cared and was trying to be nice. On the other hand, he thought she was incapable of caring for herself. And on the practical third hand, she didn't know how to put in a peephole.

She worked hard to sound gracious. "Thank you."

He stared at her, eyes narrowed. He'd probably heard her insincerity. She cleared her throat and changed the subject.

"I put all the leavery items on the register counter for you. I don't open for another hour. Anything else I can do to help?"

He finally gave her the warm smile she was longing for and *adorable* became his descriptor again, replacing bossy. He stopped by her desk and looked longingly at her cup. "Any more of that coffee?"

She looked at the now-cold dregs. "I'll get us both a fresh cup next door. Want a sticky bun to go with yours—assuming Ed has any left?"

"Sounds wonderful." His smile deepened, and she felt her heart flutter. She pictured it with wings, sort of like the Southwest Airlines logo.

She and Rog walked into the store, and she waved her hand at the treasures sitting on the counter. "Have at it. I'll be back." She started to walk down the aisle.

"Wait a minute. I've got a question." He looked from the register to the door, which was essentially looking from one end of the store to the other. "Why is your register counter in the back of the store?"

She frowned at him. "Because that's where Aunt Char had it."

He grunted as if he expected that answer. "It should be near the front."

"Because?"

"It can be seen from outside—"

"Wouldn't that attract robbery? Oh, look. Cash register. Money."

He held up a finger. "Let me finish. It discourages robbery, because it would be seen by passersby who would call the cops. And people can't shoplift as easily if they have to pass an employee on their way out."

"But it's classy back here. Like I trust my shoppers."

"You don't even know your shoppers. Which do you like? Classy or wise?"

"Can't I be classy and wise?"

"If you move it up front."

She wrinkled her nose. The expense of redesigning the store's interior on top of the pile of money needed for inventory threatened a financial bleed she wasn't sure she could afford. "A cash register at the door isn't very welcoming. Customers should see product that will lure them in, not the symbol of all the money they're going to spend in here."

"Not right at the door. You want a clear line of sight to the door. Off to the side but in the front. And don't have stuff too near the door."

"Why not?"

"You don't want to invite snatch-and-run situations, especially with all the teens jamming the boardwalk, daring each other to try something stupid."

She stared at him, frustrated. Was there nothing about Present Perfect he liked? "I'm so glad you came over."

She walked next door with her head spinning. What else

didn't she know about retail that she should?

The smell of fresh-baked goodies captured her as soon as she stepped inside, and she knew another sticky bun was just the thing to settle her tension-filled stomach. She'd work it off before noon. She bought Rog one, too.

On the sidewalk in front of Present Perfect, her hands full of coffee and food, she saw Aunt Bunny's smiling face. Today she wore a Hawaiian shirt featuring multi-colored palm trees over a pair of cropped tan pants. She wore her flip-flops with the red flowers and a red baseball cap bearing the Phillies logo, her red hair clashing in a most interesting fashion. Her red bag hung from her shoulder as usual, and she held a coffee cup.

"I see Rog is here to help with your grace-gifts problem." Aunt Bunny nodded her approval. "I tell you, Nan, he's the man for you. Oh, yes. Not that it's any of my business, of course."

"Of course." Nan smiled. "I think you're rushing the fences, Aunt Bunny. I just met the man."

Aunt Bunny merely looked smug as they walked through the store.

When Nan held out his coffee and bun, Rog took them with an appreciative sniff.

"Have a piece, Aunt Bunny." Nan tore off a piece of her bun and held it out.

"Oh, I love these buns! Ed's is the best. Thank you."

"The best," Rog agreed.

The three ate and drank contentedly. Nan was wiping the last of the crumbs from her fingers when a loud thud sounded from above. She looked up, head cocked as if waiting for another noise. Rog and Aunt Bunny stared at the ceiling too.

"You have company?" Rog put down his coffee and what remained of his bun as if readying himself for action. "Or is it Queen Elizabeth?"

"Oh, sweet Lizzie." Aunt Bunny brushed her hands on her pants. "How is that pretty girl?"

Nan continued to study the ceiling. "She still hasn't decided if she likes me."

Aunt Bunny nodded. "Still grieving. She'll come around."

"I hope." Nan narrowed her eyes as soft footfalls could be heard upstairs, followed by another thud.

"That's not the cat." Rog reached for his mic on his shoulder, ready to call for backup.

A sliding noise, like furniture being moved, sounded.

With an angry snarl, Nan smacked her coffee on the counter and bolted for the back stairs.

CHAPTER TWELVE

"Nan! Don't!" Rog grabbed for her as she raced past.

She ignored him and charged up the stairs. She could hear him muttering under his breath as he followed. She threw open the door at the top of the steps and strode into the room.

Just as she'd thought. She glared, hands on hips, at a woman in the act of moving the chairs from in front of the picture window. She was vaguely aware of Rog coming to stand beside her.

The woman turned. "Hello, Nan. Dear."

"What are you doing here, Mom?" Nan demanded. "Aside from rearranging my living

room."

Mom ignored the pique in Nan's voice and smiled. "It's such a lovely day, I just thought I'd pop down for a chat. I told you I was coming."

Right. *See you soon* in a text. Never did Nan think that message meant in the morning in Seaside, at least not until she'd heard all the commotion up here.

"Your mother?" Rog's eyebrows reached his hairline, and he took his hand from his gun.

"My mother, Elise Patterson. Mom, this is Officer Eastman."

Mom studied him without favor. "Why do you need a policeman, Nanette?"

"Hello, Ellie." Aunt Bunny peered out from behind Rog and waved.

Ellie? No one called Mom Ellie, not even Dad.

Mom spoke through a clenched jaw. "It's Elise, as you well know."

Aunt Bunny beamed, ignoring Mom's correction. "So nice to see you, Ellie. It's been a while. Char's funeral, I believe."

"Not long enough," Mom muttered in a rare show of hostility.

Nan flinched. If she'd heard, so might Aunt Bunny. She leaned in. "Mom, be nice. Please."

"Of course. I'm always nice." As if to prove her words, Mom smiled, only slightly insincere. "Nice to see you, uh, Bunny." She frowned. "Why do you let people call you Bunny?"

"I know," Aunt Bunny said cheerfully. "Bunny's a ridiculous name for an old lady, isn't it? I blame my father, who started calling me that when I was a baby. Cute then, I imagine."

Mom shook her head, whether at Aunt Bunny's name or her attitude, Nan wasn't sure. She returned to moving the chairs, no easy thing with the swivel undercarriage.

Nan eyed her mother with disfavor. "I repeat. What are you doing here?"

Mom straightened. "I came to find out what I should tell Brandon."

Nan blinked. "You tell him to find another date."

"Who's Brandon?" Aunt Bunny asked.

"The Wall Street big shot," Rog informed her.

Aunt Bunny looked impressed. "Oh, Wall Street."

Nan glared at them both, then turned back to her mother. "I cannot come to the party, Mom. I can't."

"Coming home doesn't even take two hours." Mom gave another tug on one of the chairs. "You can make that little journey to please your father and me, Nanette. I know you can." She paused in her labors to smile mistily at Nan. "It would mean so much to us."

Nan metaphorically gnashed her teeth. "It takes more like two and a half hours. Two and a half hours there and two and a half hours back and the time at the party—it's a whole day on one of my biggest weekends." How many times did she have to say it? "Mom. I. Can't."

Since it wasn't the answer she wanted, Mom ignored the comment. "Would someone please help me move these chairs?" She smiled sweetly at Rog.

Nan put a hand on his arm, though he hadn't made any move. "Don't even think about it."

Mom sighed and gave up that idea, but she clung tenaciously to the other. "Brandon is counting on you being at the party."

Nan rubbed her forehead. She and Mom had become two paths diverging in a wood, and Mom couldn't handle the divergence.

"He just got a new job at *People* magazine in their financial department. Just think. You could both be in publishing. Having things in common is so important."

"But I'm in retail!" Nan couldn't remember ever being so frustrated. Mom was worse than the leavery. "And I don't have time for *People*!"

Rog eyed her. "You don't? My mom loves *People*. My brothers and I have endured years of 'Oh, isn't that beautiful' or 'They say *that's* a best dressed? Who are they kidding?'"

"Make all the fun you want, young man." Mom pointed a finger. "Brandon has a master's degree."

Rog pressed his lips together, but Nan saw the smile struggling to escape. "How nice for him." The smile escaped.

"Mom, Rog has a law degree," Nan defended.

He put a hand on her shoulder and gave a squeeze. She marveled at the warm feeling his small appreciation and support gave her.

Mom saw the move and gave Rog her version of the evil eye. He smiled blandly and kept his hand on Nan's shoulder. Its warmth and weight felt *good*.

Mom busied herself with the furniture again, sliding an end table out of her way. "Well, Brandon can get you a job at *People*, especially with being an editor at *Pizzazz* on your resume."

Nan looked out the picture window at the ocean—strong,

sure, and calm. If the ocean could do it, so could she. Strong. Sure. Calm.

"Mom. First, I wasn't an editor at *Pizzazz*. I rewrote copy and ran errands. Second, I don't want to work at *People*. I want to work at Present Perfect. I love my job."

"Well, I don't see you working very hard." Mom's voice had become what Nan thought of as spiked. When she spoke like this, Nan pictured a mace with all the spikes sticking out, ready to impale. When she spoke this way to Dad, he left the room and the conversation. As a consequence she rarely tried it on him. Nan had never had the nerve to walk out, and as a result, had been spiked on the few occasions she and Mom had disagreed. She'd been spiked more in the last few months than in all her previous years combined.

"Your precious store isn't even open! I peeked inside before I came up here, and I saw you talking with"—Mom looked at Aunt Bunny and Rog—"these people."

Nan looked at her watch. "Yikes. Thanks for reminding me. It's almost time to open. I've got to go down."

As usual, Mom didn't hear a word that disagreed with her agenda. "Nanette. Dear. You aren't getting any younger, you know. You need a nice young man in your life." She smiled with what she probably thought looked like love but which Nan recognized as determination. "A nice young man like *Brandon*."

Embarrassed, Nan looked at Rog. What must he be thinking? When he winked at her, she felt the tension drain away. Adorable all right. And understanding.

Mom steamrolled on. "You are very lucky that a man of Brandon's caliber is willing to escort you to the party, Nanette. Not only is he Clarissa Manning's nephew, he's Daphne Jones's too."

Of keeping up with the Joneses fame. The irony was that Nan had liked Daphne Jones the few times they'd met. She was pleasant and attractive and friendly. She was also wealthy, stylish in that effortless way some women have, and powerful in the social circles Mom aspired to.

"Marrying Brandon would be a real coup." Mom looked triumphant.

Marrying him? "Mom, I haven't even met the man!"

"He'll make a wonderful son-in-law."

"Mom!"

"Isn't that jumping one's fences a bit soon, Ellie?" Aunt Bunny smiled sweetly.

Mom ignored the comment. "Oh, did I happen to mention he's wealthy?" She smiled a cat-who-ate-the-cream smile. "He's very wealthy. He lives just off Central Park."

"But does he have a TASER and a sidearm?" Rog's expression was so serious, Nan bit back a smile.

She gave him an elbow in the side even as she made her gaze at her mother as steely as she could. "Please hear me, Mom. Please! I'm not interested."

"Of course you are, Nanette. He's the best catch you'll ever find, believe me."

Was that a compliment about Brandon or a slight to her? She looked at Rog in panic, and suddenly the words spurted out as if by magic.

"I'm not interested in your best catch, Mom, because I've already found *my* best catch." She grabbed Rog's arm. "Isn't he wonderful?"

CHAPTER THIRTEEN

Rog stared down at Nan. *He* was her best catch? She stared up at him, her lovely eyes both worried and startled. Somehow, she seemed as surprised as he at her pronouncement.

Should he call her on it? Say something like, "Uh, Nan, what are you talking about?"

She blinked those great hazel eyes at him, and he kept his mouth shut. After all, she was cute. She was good company, and he liked her. A lot. Why not be a support against her mother's relentless pushing?

But he was no woman's catch. Now or ever.

Lori had taught him how dangerous getting caught was. He had finally learned to enjoy his freedom, and he did not, repeat not, want to get entangled in another relationship, no matter how cute and charming the woman.

He glanced at Mrs. Patterson. She was staring at him with something like horror, her eyes wide and her mouth open. Horror. Definitely. All that was missing was the, "No! Never him!" He wouldn't be surprised if she went all melodramatic and added a faint.

So he lived in Seaside instead of off Central Park. So he wrote tickets and arrest reports instead of financial reports. So he wore a uniform to work instead of a Brooks Brothers suit. He had a college degree. He had that law degree Nan had mentioned, and he'd gone to the Police Academy. He'd earned his blues through lots of hard work, and he was proud of what and who he was. And his work was never boring. He doubted Brandon of a magazine's financial department could say that.

He looked at Nan and raised an eyebrow. She swallowed and tried to smile. Her sheep-waiting-to-be-slaughtered look and Mrs. Patterson's not-in-this-lifetime expression cemented his decision. After all, he liked Nan, and he didn't particularly like her mother.

Note to Brandon: you do not want to be this woman's son-in-law.

He put a hand over Nan's shaking one and gave her a couple of gentle pats and a smile he tried hard to make sincere. She looked back up at him, eyes still wide with uncertainty. He had no idea what to say, so he said the first thing that came to mind.

"I've got to get back to work." He took a deep breath and forced out, "Honey."

She nodded, relief sweeping over her face, followed by that blinding smile of hers.

"I'll see you later." He emphasized the last three words.

She wrinkled her nose at him and nodded. She clearly understood that *see you later* was Rog-speak for *we have to talk*.

He dropped her hand and walked, not ran, to the stairs. He paused. "By the way, I agree with Nan. I like the chairs in front of the window, Mrs. Patterson. Makes for a cozy time watching the ocean."

He heard Nan give a choked laugh as he started down the stairs.

"Oh, Elise!" It was Aunt Bunny. "Isn't it wonderful? I knew they were meant for each other."

Fortunately, he couldn't hear Mrs. Patterson's response.

He went through the office into the store. He didn't want to leave in case Nan needed him, though she seemed to be holding her own quite well. He studied the items on the counter. Nan had put them there for him to photograph, but he didn't need to do that now that he knew what the leavery was all about.

So far, Aunt Bunny hadn't explained anything to Nan, but there'd been no time, courtesy of Mrs. Patterson's surprise visit. He didn't think she'd be here much longer, and then Aunt

Bunny could say her piece. He couldn't wait to hear how the woman framed her actions.

Aunt Bunny came through the door from the office. "Nan and Elise should be down shortly. I think I guilted Elise into looking at the store." She grinned with pride.

Rog laughed. "Good for you."

"Did you know she never went into the store when she was here to help Nan move in? It's like if she doesn't look at Present Perfect, it doesn't exist, and Nan will go back to her old life."

"But she won't." Rog understood Nan's need to stand up to her mother about the store, because he'd had to do the same about being on the force. Facing down parents who loved you and cared for you was a hard task, but choosing a career wasn't the parents' job, no matter how good their intentions.

More footsteps, and Nan came into the store looking back over her shoulder. "Come on, Mom." Her voice was nervous and uncertain.

Mrs. Patterson was apparently stalled in the office. "I have to get back home," she said. "So much to do for the party."

But there was time to rearrange Nan's apartment without permission?

"Ten minutes, Mom."

Couldn't the woman hear the emotion in Nan's voice? Didn't she understand how much this meant to her daughter?

"Ten minutes isn't that much to ask, is it, Elise?" Aunt Bunny called sweetly. "After all, it's the career your daughter has chosen, and she wants to share it with you."

Mrs. Patterson appeared in the doorway and shot an ugly look at the old woman, who pretended not to notice.

"You'll love her inventory and her eye for display." Aunt Bunny continued, and Rog had to smile. The spunky lady knew how to manipulate—and irritate. "She's very gifted, but of course you already know that."

With that final turn of the knife, Aunt Bunny picked up one of the pressed-flower pictures and pretended to study it.

Nan looked at her mother. "Come on, Mom. Please?"

Mrs. Patterson blew out a mighty sigh. "Oh, all right. Five minutes. Then I must get on my way."

She wasn't exactly ungracious, but she definitely wasn't gracious as she walked the aisles. Rog watched Nan as she watched her mother. He might not be her catch, though he was certain he'd be a better one for her than Brandon ever would, but he did care when she was hurt.

~ * ~

Nan watched her mom nervously. She wanted so badly for her to like Present Perfect and tell her she was doing a good job that her stomach ached. She feared those words weren't going to be spoken.

Nan tried to see the store through Mom's eyes. It was hard, since it meant so much to her—a career she enjoyed, a connection to Aunt Char, an answer to a desperate prayer. To Mom it meant disappointment, dissension, and lost dreams.

The barn-siding walls were stained a medium brown, and display shelves of the same shade held her stock. Sure, many of the items were related to the shore, but they were attractive display pieces to put in one's home, either here at the shore or inland as a reminder of a wonderful vacation week. Beautiful seashells sat in baskets beside signs that read *Beach Time* and *Down the Shore*. There were prints of sand dunes and Adirondack chairs under beach umbrellas, not that anyone actually took an Adirondack chair to the beach. Small lamps with seashell bases cast soft light on displays of frames and pottery, hand painted tiles, and framed maps of the island. Ceramic starfish, wooden seagulls, and glass dolphins sat in sand scattered artistically on one shelf.

Mom walked around the store with all the enthusiasm of a kid in a doctor's office knowing a shot awaits. She frowned and looked at Nan. "Where are the sweatshirts and sunglasses?"

Nan felt hope at the question. Mom had noticed Present Perfect was different. "There are lots of nice shops with stuff like that all up and down the boardwalk. Aunt Char made

Present Perfect special, and I want to keep it that way."

Still frowning, Mom continued walking up and down the aisles, examining the shelves and the goods. Nan hated that her stomach was in turmoil as she waited to hear Mom's assessment.

Aunt Bunny sidled up to her. "It's a wonderful store, Nan. Whatever Elise says, it's wonderful. Char had great taste, and you have the same gene." She tugged her red tote higher on her shoulder. "I need to talk to you, but not now. I've got to go. I've a meeting at eleven. I want to beat Alana there." Her eyes sparkled with the thought.

Nan laughed at an image of Aunt Bunny in her Hawaiian shirt and red flip-flops sitting in a meeting beside the impeccably tailored Alana. She leaned in and kissed the woman's soft cheek. "Have fun."

Aunt Bunny snorted. "I doubt it."

"Hey, you the owner?"

Nan turned to find a lanky guy slouching beside her with dark hair that needed a barber. "I am."

A goofy, yet charming, smile was accompanied by a big hand reaching to shake. "I'm Mooch Traylor. I'm hoping you want to hire me for the summer."

"Mooch?" She was aware of Rog eyeing the boy.

"Yeah. My mama says I'll mooch food off anyone." His goofy grin came again. "And she's right. I will."

Nan couldn't resist grinning back. "And why do I want to hire you, Mooch?"

"'Cause I can carry stuff for you, and I can work lots of hours, and my landlord says I gotta get a job."

As he spoke, he fiddled with the items sitting on the closest counter. When he stopped, Nan stared. He'd rearranged things, and somehow the counter looked more inviting, the groupings warmer, more artful.

"How did you do that?" Nan pointed to the counter.

He followed her finger. "Do what?"

"You rearranged everything."

"I did? Did I mess it up?" He looked stricken. "I always do

stuff like that. It drives my mom nuts. How was it before? I'll put it back."

Nan turned to the counter opposite, where plates with paintings of colorful shore birds on them sat in piles, watercolor pictures leaned against the wall, and beside them, vases and wooden decoys stood next to a pair of sailboats of differing heights. "Rearrange them."

Mooch looked at the collection. "Not bad. Not good, but not bad. You have any of those picture supports? You know, those little tripod things?"

Nan ran to the office, passing Rog, who was leaning against the register counter, ankles crossed, arms folded.

"Problem?" he asked.

She paused at the storeroom door. "I've got exactly the kid I need, I think. I just hope he doesn't have a record or a drug habit or something equally undesirable."

She grabbed some easels and hurried back to the store just in time to hear Rog say, "*Hey, you the owner?* Geez, kid, where are your manners?"

"What?" Mooch looked confused.

"How about, 'Excuse me, miss, are you the owner?' "

Mooch shrugged. "Hey. I lack class. Who cares?"

"I do." Rog's look was stern.

Mooch appeared unaffected.

Rog glanced at Nan and went back to leaning on the counter.

She handed Mooch a fistful of easels as she wondered at Rog's interference over something so petty. The kid was seventeen or eighteen. She was pleased he hadn't said, "Yo!"

Mooch took the easels and started moving things. While he worked, Nan followed her mother with her eyes. Mom stopped her wandering and picked up a lighthouse with a switch. She flicked it, and a light at the top of its tower came on. She glanced at Nan as she turned the light off and put the lighthouse down. She moved on without comment.

So far, there were no unexplained items this morning, and Nan was very glad. She shuddered at the thought of explaining leavery to Mom.

"Done." Mooch stepped back. "That's as good as I can do with what's here." He looked around him. "I could do better if you let me move stuff around, like from there to here, you know?"

She nodded. She knew. She studied the rearranged shelf. "Very nice, Mooch. You're good. Come on back to the office, and we can get your paperwork started."

"I'm hired?" The goofy grin appeared yet again.

"We'll see." She smiled noncommittally while hoping he would work out.

They turned toward the office, or at least Nan did. Mooch was rooted to the spot, staring at the front door. Nan turned and saw Tammy in her blue Present Perfect shirt walking toward them.

"Whoa." Mooch leaned toward Nan. "She come with the place?"

Nan nodded.

"Cool."

Tammy came close, and Nan swore she could hear Mooch hyperventilating.

"Tammy, this is Mooch Traylor. He's applied for a job here. Mooch, Tammy can answer any of your questions if I'm not around."

Tammy smiled. "Mooch, huh? Interesting name."

"It's really Daniel," he mumbled, suddenly shy.

"Okay." Tammy looked to the back of the store. "I see Officer Studly is here, serving and protecting."

Nan watched Rog glance in their direction, indicating he'd heard.

"You always have a cop here?" Mooch asked.

"He's trying to solve the mystery of the leavery." She watched Tammy sashay toward Rog and wasn't surprised to see him start for the office door and escape.

"I'll talk to you later," he called. "Bye." He was gone before Tammy reached him.

Tammy sagged against the counter, a pout marring her

pretty face as she watched him disappear.

Mooch watched her and sighed. "He's a good guy, but not for her. Too old. Now me on the other hand..."

Nan looked at him with surprise and concern. "You know the officer?"

"Yeah, but don't worry. Not in a professional capacity. He's my landlord."

"Really? I didn't know he took in boarders."

Mooch looked slightly uncomfortable. "Well, he's not really my landlord because I don't pay rent. But I do live at his house, and he did tell me I needed a job. In fact, he suggested I come here."

Nan studied the boy. No wonder Rog was correcting him earlier. "I'm assuming that means he trusts you."

He shrugged. "In spite of everything."

Nan grew cautious again. "What do you mean?"

"He used to go with my sister and got me in the split."

Nan blinked. "You're Lori's brother?"

"He told you about her?" Mooch seemed surprised. "Huh."

"She broke up with him when he decided to become a cop."

"Yeah. Not her finest moment. I have to ask myself if she's going to dump me when I become a cop—which I plan to be."

Nan laughed. She liked the kid. "I don't think you can dump brothers. They're yours for life."

"Cool. What's leavery?"

As Nan explained, Mooch followed Tammy with his eyes.

"So Rog stopped in to see if anything else showed up," she finished. "And photograph what's here." Though, as she thought back, she hadn't seen a camera and to her knowledge, he hadn't taken a single picture.

"Cool."

"And I don't encourage staff fraternization."

Mooch nodded, not the least bit disconcerted by the abrupt change of subject. "At least not at the store." He grinned. "You won't know what happens away from work, right? But I get it. It could get sticky."

"Yes, it could." She turned toward the back. "Tammy, please bring out that order of ceramic angels and hang them on the Christmas tree."

"Here, let me help." Mooch hurried after her.

Mom walked up the center aisle and stopped beside Nan. "I don't think you should hire that boy, Nanette. I see trouble there."

Nan frowned. "He's fine, Mom. Rog recommended him."

"Oh. Well."

It wasn't *oh, well, then it's okay*. It was definitely *oh, well, then I'm right. You're in for trouble.*

"Look how he reorganized the shelf." Nan pointed.

Mom looked but said nothing.

Nan sighed. There would be no approval coming for Mooch, for the store, for Rog, or for her. If only it didn't hurt so much.

CHAPTER FOURTEEN

Late that afternoon, the raucous sound of the buzzer at the back door made Nan smile. He was here.

"Come in!" She stood and stretched, happy to leave the numbers she was working with, and headed for the door. She pulled it wide, and there Rog was. How ridiculous to feel this rush of pleasure at the sight of him. He was just a guy, and she'd only known him for two days. Really not even two days. Still, she wondered if she'd ever felt this excited to see Tyler.

He wore a T-shirt that had seen better days and a pair of paint-spattered knee-length shorts and was loaded down with a pouch of tools in one hand and an electric drill clutched in the other. A white painter's cap sat on his head.

She grinned at him.

He frowned at her. "Why did you open the door?"

She blinked. "To let you in."

"But you didn't check—"

"—to see who it was. Yeah, yeah. But I was expecting you."

"But you didn't know it was me."

She waved his comment away and stepped back to let him in. She eyed the pouch and the drill. "You look like a man with serious intentions."

He gave her a slow smile. "You have no idea."

She swallowed. Was he flirting with her? Yowzah!

He turned a little pink, blinked, and plain Rog was back, not as all-business as Rog the Cop, but not at all flirty. He walked to her desk and unloaded on top of the catalogs.

"I have another load in the car." He strode to the still open door. "Back in a minute. And close the door behind me."

She did as told, leaning against the door, listening to the rapid beat of her heart. Nuts. She was nuts! But he was adorable.

The buzzer sounded.

"Yes?" she called.

"It's me."

"Who's me?"

"Rog." She heard the smile in his voice. "Roger Smedley Eastman."

"Smedley? Your middle name is Smedley?"

"My mom's maiden name."

She grinned. "How do I know it's really you?"

"Because I say so?"

"Anyone could say so. It could be someone imitating you. Prove it's you."

He was quiet for a moment. "You like Ferris wheels and I don't."

"Proof if I ever heard it." She opened the door.

He had a bag bulging with unidentifiable objects clasped in his fist.

"What's all this stuff?"

He walked to her desk, added the bag to the jumble already there, and pulled out a box. "Your peephole for one thing." He held the box toward her as if to prove his words.

"You going to install it now?"

"Is that a problem?"

"Dinner's in the oven upstairs. It's almost ready."

"Do I have five minutes?"

She nodded. "Five minutes."

He opened the box and lifted out a screen about the size of a cell phone. A small camera followed.

She eyed the things with interest. "Very cool. I was expecting a fisheye lens thing."

"Old-fashioned. We're going for high tech." He measured and put an X in the middle of the door.

"Am I supposed to see out of that?" She went up on tiptoe.

He looked from the X to her, then waved her over. "Stand here." Another X, this one at her height instead of his.

His drill whirred as he made a small round hole and then enlarged it to the size of the tube connected to the camera. In no time, she had an electronic peephole that showed her a picture of whoever was outside the door.

Rog went outside and pulled the door shut. "Push the button on the screen," he called.

She did and there he was, clear as day.

"I love it!" she told him as he came back in. "I feel so much safer already. Now come on upstairs. Dinner's got to be ready." She grabbed his tool pouch to carry up and was surprised at the weight. "What have you got in here?"

He held out the drill. "Take this. I'll take the pouch." He followed her up the stairs, the pouch in one hand, a paint can in the other. He deposited everything just inside the bedroom.

They sat at Aunt Char's antique table, which Nan had set with Pimpernel placemats that had pictures of roosters on them. She added the rooster plates she found in the armoire Aunt Char kept her entertaining supplies in. The napkins were black and white checked to match the border on the placemats, and the glasses sported black rims. The red Gerbera daisies she'd found at the supermarket added a splash of color.

"Roosters, huh?" Rog took his seat.

"I guess Aunt Char saw them as a break from seashells and beach scenes."

"They're fine, but it's what goes on them that counts, and it smells wonderful." His smile only deepened as she served him roasted chicken, broccoli and cheese casserole, and a baked potato.

After he said grace, she helped herself to a spoonful of cranberry relish for her chicken. "I didn't have any leavery today."

He looked pleased. "Good."

"Do you think it's finally stopped?"

"The giver has probably seen the light now that you've gotten a cop involved. This chicken's great."

"Thanks. So I've got what? Presents left by an unidentified hyperactive secret pal?"

He added more sour cream to his potato. "What's a secret pal?"

"You know. People draw names, and for a year, everyone gives gifts to the person they drew, but they don't reveal themselves until the year is up."

"Like birthday and Christmas presents?"

"And any other day you feel like. Valentine's or Fourth of July. Unbirthday."

"And where do you get the names to give these secret presents to?"

"Usually it's someone in a group of friends or a club. We used to do it in Girl Scouts when I was a kid."

"Ha! I knew it. It's a girl thing."

Nan sat up straight, taken with a thought. "So the perpetrator is female?" Had they just eliminated half the world, give or take a few million?

Rog nodded. "They're female type gifts. If a guy was leaving stuff, it'd be tools or baseball mitts or a couple of universal TV remotes."

Nan laughed as she rose to clear the table. When she offered him double chocolate brownies with ice cream, he couldn't stop smiling. After he polished dessert off, he sat back with his coffee in hand.

They fell silent, smiling at each other until Nan had to move so she could breathe again. She jumped to her feet and grabbed the coffee carafe. "More?"

"Thanks." He pushed his cup toward her. "That was a wonderful meal. The chicken was some of the best I've ever had.'"

She delighted in his praise. "My mom's recipe."

His smile faded, and he became much too somber. "Speaking of your mother."

I'm not interested in your best catch, Mom, because I've already found my best catch. Isn't he wonderful?

Her stomach cramped and her face flushed. Dinner had

been so pleasant, she'd dared hope he'd forgotten about her ridiculous assertion, but no such luck.

~ * ~

Rog watched Nan's cheeks turn scarlet. He hated to upset her, especially after she'd fed him that great dinner, but her comment had to be addressed before it became the elephant in the room. He didn't want times with her to be awkward. He liked her too much. She was sweet and kind and cute. She'd even given Mooch a job.

But he wasn't anyone's catch. He didn't want to be anyone's catch. He wasn't some fish waiting to be reeled in. When she'd spoken this morning, he could almost feel her tug her line to set the hook in him. It was all he could do to not spit out the imaginary barb while he could, but one look at her mother's sour face had kept him quiet.

"I'm sorry, Rog." She traced the rooster's tail on her placemat with her finger rather than look at him. "I don't know what came over me."

He knew. Her mother.

She shook her head, her expression one of disbelief. "I don't know where those words came from. They just popped out."

"Pressure of the moment."

Nan sighed. "She loves me, you know."

There was something sweet about her defending the infuriating woman. "Shouldn't love be encouraging?"

Nan gave a little laugh. "She thought she was encouraging. She wants what she thinks is best for me."

"And that's Brandon."

"And *Pizzazz.*"

"I'd find her pushing very—" Lots of words sat on the tip of his tongue, words like infuriating or interfering, but he caught himself. The woman was, after all, Nan's mother, and aggravating as he found her, Nan cared for her, so he settled for the rather bland "—frustrating."

"Oh, it is, believe me, but that's no excuse for what I said. So she pushed too hard. So I was upset and at my wits' end. A lie's a lie, even if it's only by implication. You probably won't believe me, but I try hard not to lie. I work really hard not to even exaggerate." Her voice shook.

He tried not to lie, too, and he had to admit that sometimes he failed. He sighed. "It's okay. I'm not mad." And he wasn't, at least not any more.

"It's not okay, and I was wrong, and you can be mad if you need to be."

He reached for her hand, and she gave it to him. It was so small in his. He ran his thumb back and forth, back and forth over her soft skin. "We can't let her believe an untrue thing. It's not right."

"I know, but confessing my stupidity will be so embarrassing!"

Rog doubted Joan of Arc looked that pitiful when she went to the stake. He gave her hand a squeeze. "We'll figure this out."

"We will?" She stared at him with such hope his stomach cramped. "How?"

"I haven't the vaguest idea."

For a minute, they just smiled at each other. She really was sweet. Maybe a bit truth-challenged, but sweet.

"I've tried so hard to be a good Christian in front of my family," she said. "They think I'm nuts for believing. They're convinced I'll become a fanatic and end up drinking grape Kool-Aid in some faraway jungle somewhere."

He held out his other hand, and she laid hers in it. He held his up, and she fit the base of her palm against the base of his. Her fingertips reached just past his first knuckle. He slid his palm down and their fingers laced.

"I grew up in a Christian family," Rog said. "I can't remember when I didn't believe in Jesus."

Nan nodded. "I was never even in a church until my roommate got married when I was twenty-one. I was in a Bible study at college and had been for a couple of years by then, but not an organized church. It was Aunt Char who told me I needed to find one and get involved when I finished school."

Rog looked into her serious hazel eyes. "I think I would have liked Aunt Char."

"You would have. She was wonderful. The thing I appreciated most about her was her faith. She loved God and wasn't afraid to tell you so. In fact, she spent my first summer here telling me how much God loved me. It made me so uncomfortable, I wanted to go home half the time. The other half, I was having so much fun being in Seaside that I couldn't leave."

"And you came back."

"Every summer. I decided my third summer I wanted what she had, and I became a Christ follower. I met Tyler at the Christian fellowship group on campus I started attending after I believed. When I introduced him to my parents, they were so relieved he was normal that they really liked him. Until he dumped me. Then he was this hypocrite of a Christian who said one thing while he lived another. 'He took your good years!' my father roared. Like I have no good ones left. I think one of the reasons Mom is so set on fixing me up with Brandon is that they're afraid of the man I might select."

"Too religious. Another perceived hypocrite."

"Right. Too fanatical. Like my father told me once, not everyone likes church as much as I do."

"A true statement, no doubt." He smiled at her. "Know what I think?"

She shook her head.

"I think you're secretly relieved you can't get away the weekend of the Fourth. You're spared the Brandon ordeal."

She actually grinned. "If I could get away, and if you weren't busy keeping Seaside safe for democracy, I'd take you as my date, not Brandon. At least I'd know what I was getting, and original context aside, you definitely are a good catch."

"Want to tell Lori for me?"

"Forget her." Nan pulled a hand free and made an erasing motion. "She's no longer a person of interest."

And with surprise, Rog realized she wasn't.

Nan pulled her other hand free and started clearing the table. He stood to help her. He wasn't sure they'd resolved the *catch* problem, but at least it was no longer an issue between the two of them. That was a good first step.

When the dishwasher was loaded, she turned to him. "You won't finish painting tonight, will you?"

"Not a chance."

"How about dinner tomorrow?"

He grinned. "This is a great gig."

He started for the bedroom, then stopped in the doorway, turned, and eyed her. He leaned into the jamb and crossed one foot over the other at the ankles. Very Joe Cool if he did say so.

"By the way, I like church." And with a wink, he turned away, savoring her startled look.

CHAPTER FIFTEEN

When Rog disappeared into the bedroom, Nan dropped into her chair at the table. Oh, boy, was she in trouble.

When she'd moved here, she told herself no men. She'd promised herself. No men, just lots of hard work. So much was at stake here. She had to prove herself, and that would take every ounce of strength and every minute of her time.

In just two days, Rog was making a lie of that plan. The first time she'd seen him walking into the store all starchy and professional, she'd felt it, whatever *it* was. Love at first sight? Or at least lots of like at first glance. It was as if he were the biggest gift of all in this whole leavery thing, and God had sent him. Talk about grace-gifts.

Not that he returned her feelings. Sure, he'd flirted here and there, but he always pulled back. The brutal specter of his failed romance with Lori clung to him like a bad odor to a pup who'd tried to be friends with a skunk. And she'd made him even more hesitant with her stupid catch statement.

She sighed and rose. She'd survived Tyler; she would survive Rog. She would.

Lord, I will, right?

She ran the water in the kitchen sink until it was as hot as she could stand it, then wet the dishcloth. She squeezed it dry and wiped the placemats clean. She dried them with a paper towel and carried them to the drawer in the armoire. With all the wonderful grace-gifts she'd received from Aunt Char, she neither needed nor wanted the leavery items.

A thought slid through her mind and she glanced toward

the bedroom. When she got frustrated with the leavery, she needed to remember that if not for it, she might never have met Rog. Instead of griping about all that stuff, maybe she should be thanking the Lord.

~ * ~

Rog grinned to himself as he prepared the bedroom for painting. Teasing Nan was the most fun he'd had in—well, he couldn't remember how long.

He studied the pink walls. Usually he didn't mind pink. It was a girl color for sure, but it could be pretty. He liked it on things like roses and babies and little princesses like his nieces. But this pink, no way. Even in a room where you had your eyes shut most of the time, it was grating. For a woman of taste like Aunt Char, she'd sure fallen off the wagon with this shade.

"I hope you don't mind sleeping on the sofa for a few nights," he called as he tested the weight of the bureau. Heavy!

Nan appeared in the door and watched as he manhandled the bureau away from the wall inch by tiny inch. "I don't mind the sofa. Do you want Mooch to help you move stuff?"

He hadn't wanted to ask. After all, Mooch worked for her. "That'd be great if you can spare him."

"I'm going down in a minute, and I'll send him up." She started to turn away, then looked back. "Promise me you'll wait for him. I don't want any ruptured discs. I don't think my workman's comp insurance covers friendly house painters."

She was worried about him. It was stupid, but he felt somehow blessed.

She looked around the room. "You've got to move all the furniture, don't you? Even the bed."

"I have to get to the walls behind stuff."

"Right. Will I be able to get to my clothes?"

"The closet, no problem until we have to empty it to paint. For other things, I'd suggest you get a couple of days' worth and store them somewhere where they won't get dusty or paint spattered. I'm about to cover everything with tarps."

Her shoulders slumped. "This is going to be a bigger deal than I thought."

He grinned. "Just think about the end product: a lovely room you'll be happy to go to sleep in every night."

She left, and a few minutes later, Mooch appeared. "The boss lady said I'm to help you move stuff." He seemed less than enthusiastic.

"Ever paint a room before?" Rog was pretty sure of the answer.

"You kidding? That's what you hire people for."

"You've been hired."

"But not for painting. I'm an artistic consultant."

"You're a stock boy and general dogsbody, and you won't be painting. You're being used for hard labor." He looked at the lanky kid and grinned. "We're bulking you up for the ladies."

Mooch got a faraway look. "Lady. Singular."

Rog rolled his eyes. "Let me guess. The beauteous Tammy?"

"She is beautiful, isn't she?"

Rog expected the kid to start drooling any minute. He snapped his fingers. "Yo, Romeo. Stay with me. The sooner we're finished here, the sooner you can go swoon over her."

"Ha, ha. I don't swoon." He grinned. "But I do pant a bit."

Rog laughed and threw Mooch the car keys. "There are several canvas tarps in the back. Bring them up, will you?"

While Mooch clomped down the stairs, Rog removed pictures and carried them into the living room, where he propped them against the wall. He was resting the last one carefully when he heard thumps on the back door and the buzzer squawked.

"Who's there?" Nan called.

Before he could remind her to push the button on her new electronic peephole, he heard her laugh. "I see you, Mooch." And the back door opened. When Mooch came upstairs with the tarps in his arms, Nan followed.

Her face glowed with pleasure. "I love it!"

He grinned at her, his shoulders straightening a bit. Nothing like impressing a lady, especially when it was so easy a task.

She fled downstairs, and he turned to find Mooch staring at him with an I-don't-believe-it look. "What?"

"And you have the nerve to give me grief. Your own tongue is hanging out a mile."

"Is not."

"Is so."

"Is not."

Mooch shook his head in disgust. "Deny it all you want. You think she's hot."

Rog swallowed. "She's a very attractive young woman. Very nice."

Mooch hooted and Rog squirmed. Before he could decide how to deny his attraction to Nan with any plausibility, the back door buzzer blatted again. A minute passed, and Nan didn't answer it. The buzzer sounded again.

"Want me to get it?" Mooch looked anxious to do anything but move furniture.

"You're cheap labor. I'll get it while you put the night tables in the living room. Remember to unplug the lamps and move them separately."

"You'd think he thought I was dumb," Mooch told the air. "Unplug the lamps. Geez!"

Rog grinned, hurried down the stairs, and hit the button on the viewing screen. An older man in a dress shirt, his tie pulled loose and his top shirt button undone, stood outside. Rog pulled the door open. "May I help you?"

"Oh." The man was clearly thrown off stride at the sight of Rog. "I thought this was Present Perfect."

"It is." Rog pointed to the name painted on the door.

"I was expecting my daughter."

Rog's finely honed deductive skills kicked in. "Mr. Patterson?" He shot out his hand. "Pleased to meet you. I'm Rog Eastman."

Mr. Patterson blinked and slowly extended his arm.

"Dad?"

Both men turned as Nan came into the storeroom. She hurried to her visitor with a welcoming smile and gave him a hug. He bent and kissed her cheek.

"This is a surprise." Her happy expression was replaced by anxiety. "Is something wrong? Is Mom okay?"

Mr. Patterson patted her arm. "Don't worry. Everything's fine. I didn't mean to scare you." His eyes slued toward Rog. "Um, can we talk somewhere, sweetheart? Somewhere private?"

Rog watched Nan look at him apologetically and bit back a smile at her pained expression. Protective fathers were the same everywhere.

"Hey, Rog!" Mooch appeared at the top of the steps. "What do you want your child labor to do next?"

Nan stepped to the bottom of the stairs. "Forget Rog, Mooch. I'll take *my* child labor in Present Perfect while I visit with my dad." She signaled to him, and the kid cooperatively thumped his way down to the office.

Nan indicated the store. "Go help Tammy and Ingrid."

Mooch gave a nod. "Yes, ma'am. As you wish, ma'am." He looked at Rog. "You gotta love a strong woman."

Without pausing for breath, he stuck out his hand to Mr. Patterson. "Since these people haven't the manners to introduce me before they send me to the mines, I'll do it myself. Mooch Traylor. I work here. Child labor."

"Mooch," Rog warned. The kid must have forgotten to take his Ritalin.

Mooch made believe he didn't hear. "When my dead body shows up, bring charges against these two for youth abuth." He grinned. "Say youth abuse fast three times and see what you get." He laughed. "Youth abuse. Youth abuth. Youth abuth." He leaned in and stage-whispered to Rog, "You look awesome. Nice way to impress the father of your crush."

Rog glanced down himself all the way to his laceless, paint-spattered sneakers. Sartorial splendor all right.

Mooch gave his goofy grin. "It's got to be embarrassing that I look better than you."

With a satisfied smile that he'd wreaked enough havoc for one evening, Mooch disappeared into the store.

Rog glanced at Nan, who had a little half smile as she watched the boy go. Sure, she could think he was funny. She wasn't responsible for him. That would be Rog. Being around the boy was like watching a super ball ricochet wildly around the room, waiting for it to bounce into an irreplaceable antique and shatter it. No wonder Lori was happy to pack him off to Seaside for the summer.

But the kid sure could be funny.

Nan turned to Rog, looked him up and down, and laughed. "He's right, you know. Street person."

"I'll have you know I worked hard for this look. Spent hours in front of the mirror mixing and matching. Years in the field splattering the shoes and shorts. The shirt is just a victim of natural attrition."

Mr. Patterson frowned and cleared his throat.

Nan let her smile fade. "Um, Dad, would you like to walk around the store while you're here?"

The look of hope on her face touched Rog. He watched Mr. Patterson shake his head and saw the hope drain away. She caught him watching her and shrugged.

"Come on upstairs, Dad. We can sit and talk there."

Nan led the way with Mr. Patterson following. Rog brought up the rear.

Mr. Patterson looked over his shoulder. "Um..."

Nan didn't miss a beat. "He's painting my bedroom, Dad. He has to come up."

"Oh."

As soon as they entered the living room, they all but tripped over the pair of bedside tables in the middle of the floor. The bedside lamps sat like tipsy friends in the middle of the sofa.

Rog shook his head. "Sorry. My fault. I didn't tell him to put them against the wall." He muscled the tables out of the way and put the lamps on them.

"So you're working for Nan?" Mr. Patterson asked as he took a seat in one of the chairs by the window.

Rog bit back a smile. "No, sir, not working for her exactly. I'm helping her out with some painting."

"He's safe, Dad," Nan called from the kitchen where she was pouring three glasses of iced tea. "You don't have to worry."

"Of course I worry. It's what parents do, especially about their baby girls."

Right then, Rog decided he liked Mr. Patterson.

After handing her father his iced tea, Nan wandered to the bedroom door and glanced at the canvas-covered rug and furnishings and the bare walls. "Looks strange."

Rog stood beside her. Mooch had done a lot more than move the night tables. "Just wait. I haven't begun to do strange yet." He put a hand on her shoulder and squeezed.

She glanced back at him, her eyes unhappy. Two parents in one day had to be overwhelming.

"Want me to stay with you," he asked softly, "or would you rather I disappear? I can close the door and work. Or I can go home."

She turned and grabbed his hand. "Stay. Please."

He nodded. It was what he wanted, too. Protect and serve.

She walked to the sofa, pulling Rog behind her. "Rog offered to paint for me, Dad, and I'm so glad, because I wouldn't be able to get to it before late fall. Plus he knows what he's doing, and I don't." She sat and he sat beside her.

"Worked my way through college as a painter." Okay, Rog knew he said that to impress Mr. Patterson with his college degree. Petty but satisfying. Just because he looked like a bum...

Mr. Patterson barely glanced at him before he focused on Nan. "You're saying the store is that demanding?"

She nodded. "More demanding than *Pizzazz*."

"Then you need a break—" he began, but she raised a hand to cut him off.

"No break, Dad. I can't. Not this time of year."

"I don't know, Nan. You had such a good job, a good salary and benefits, and you threw it all away."

"I like it so much better here at Present Perfect. In fact, even with all the pressure and work, I love it."

He still looked unconvinced. "Your mother called me today, nearly hysterical."

Nan frowned. "Over me? There's nothing to get hysterical over, Dad. Believe me. I'm fine. I'm happy. I'm where I want to be."

Mr. Patterson looked at Rog who was still holding hands with Nan. Really, it was Nan hanging onto him, but he didn't mind in the least. Rog offered the man a pleasant smile.

Mr. Patterson frowned and looked back at his daughter. "She's worried about the way you're treating poor Brandon. I have to admit, I'm surprised after the way Tyler hurt you."

Nan blinked. "How am I treating Brandon? And what's Tyler got to do with him?"

"Oh, I know you're not engaged yet, but according to your mother, it's on the horizon. And where would she get this news but from you?"

Nan gripped Rog more tightly. "Dad, I have never even met Brandon."

"Of course you have. You both work in New York."

Frustration oozed from her. "New York City is huge, millions of people. We don't all know each other."

"I know that," Mr. Patterson began.

But Nan bulldozed on. "I have never met Brandon, never ever, and I've told Mom repeatedly I don't *want* to meet him."

Mr. Patterson looked baffled. "You've never met him?"

"Never. Mom invited him to the Fourth party so I could meet him."

"But you've never met him, not even once."

"And I probably never will. I'm not coming to the party."

He glanced again at Rog, his frown renewed. "She told me you've taken up with someone unsatisfactory down here, and you're throwing Brandon over."

"Untrue, Dad, on both counts."

"Then who's he?" He nodded at Rog.

"Roger Eastman, cop." Rog spoke brusquely, tired of being frowned at.

"And law school graduate," Nan added.

Something in Rog warmed as she once again defended him. "I'm a police officer, Mr. Patterson. I'm proud to be one. I don't think anyone wants to say that makes me unsatisfactory."

"No, no, of course not." Mr. Patterson backtracked quickly. He ran a hand through his hair. "I'm confused."

"Let me explain." Nan sat up straight, but she still gripped Rog's hand tightly. "I do not know Brandon. For some reason, Mom has decided he's a good man for me, but he isn't. She wants me to come for the Fourth of July party, but I can't. She thinks I should go back to *Pizzazz*, but I won't."

She looked at Rog. "Can you think of anything else?"

The fact that she was turning to him didn't strike him as strange—which was in itself strange. They'd only met yesterday, but it was like they'd known each other forever. "Anything else?" He thought for a moment, then shook his head. "That about sums it up."

"Then who are you dating, Nan?" Mr. Patterson asked. "Who's your mother worried about?"

Brows raised, Rog looked at Nan, who looked back with a crooked smile. Close as they'd become, they'd never dated, and now didn't seem the proper moment to ask for their first date. Maybe she'd count the dinner with Aunt Bunny.

She turned to her father. "I'm dating Rog," she said without batting an eye. "We went out to dinner last night, and he's going to be my plus one at a formal event Thursday."

CHAPTER SIXTEEN

Rog felt Mr. Patterson's dagger gaze skewer him, but he didn't return the man's look. He was too busy eyeing Nan, who was equally busy not looking at him.

A formal event Thursday night? As in the day after tomorrow? As in he would be expected to wear a tux? And he was learning about it through an announcement to her father. Would it have been too much trouble for her to actually invite him? *Say, Rog, I have tickets to this formal event. Would you like to go as my date?*

Then he could politely say thanks, but no. He didn't like formal events. They made him uncomfortable, like all the elegant people knew what to do and they'd forgotten to tell him. He was comfortable in his uniform, in his painting grubbies, in casual clothes. He'd managed his tux well at his brothers' weddings, but then he'd known what was expected of him. Seat the little old ladies. Smile when the groom of the day said, "I do."

But a formal event? Even the word *event* made him prickly all over. Not a dance where he could make believe he was shuffling around a basketball court in time with the music. Not a dinner where he would presumably get better-than-normal food, which he would enjoy eating.

An *event*.

Maybe it didn't really matter whether he went. Rather, it mattered that her father thought they were going, thought they were an item. If he thought they were going, then her mother would think they were going, and Brandon would become a non-problem. So would the conflict over the party.

Maybe. Or maybe not. Maybe it would intensify that problem. He could imagine her mother saying, "What? You have time for an event but not my party?"

When he was growing up wondering how he could serve the Lord and mankind, being used as a buffer between a woman and her parents hadn't been remotely on his radar. And what in the world was wrong with him that going to a formal event was scarier than wearing a bulletproof vest and facing bad guys with big guns?

He waited for the resentment at being trapped into something he didn't want to do, but none surfaced. Instead he found himself thinking about Nan in a formal gown, and the thought of an evening with her seemed worth the rental price and discomfort of his monkey suit. With her at his side, he'd smile at everyone all evening, and maybe no one would realize how uncomfortable he was. Maybe, just maybe, he'd even enjoy himself.

Quickly, his duty schedule ran through his mind. He should be off duty at four on Thursday, barring any unforeseen catastrophe, always a possibility in his profession. Nan would have to learn that truth—of schedules being wrecked at a moment's notice—if they ever formed an actual relationship. But if everything at work went as usual, he would be free to go.

"There's a gala to dedicate the new hospital wing," Nan told her father.

A gala? That sounded even scarier than an event. Fancier. Classier.

"I've been asked to represent Aunt Char, who had something to do with—" She circled her hand to convey uncertainty, "—something somehow."

Mr. Patterson looked interested. "The Buchanan Children's Place?"

Nan nodded. "How do you know about that?"

"My architectural firm bid on the job at Char's request, but they selected a local group. I drove past the building on my way here. It looks good, much as I hate to admit it." He studied Nan. "So you're going to take Char's place."

Nan made a face. "I could never do that, but we're going to the evening in her name." She gave Rog an ingratiating smile, then turned back to her father as if she hadn't told another giant whopper.

What was he supposed to do with an adorable pixie he thought was cute and interesting but who led her parents to believe in a relationship that didn't exist?

He glanced at their hands clasped between them. Or did it?

~ * ~

Nan waited for Rog to say, "We're going to an event? A gala? Unh-unh. You may be going, but I'm not."

Instead she felt him running his thumb around and around the back of her hand. It was so soothing. Surely it meant he wasn't going to tell Dad that he hadn't known a thing about the gala until ten seconds ago. She began to relax a little, and the gala event she'd been dreading became something that would be fun. If Rog was with her, how could it be otherwise?

"Stop! Stop right there! Get back here!" The shouts came from downstairs and sounded like Mooch. "You take that back!"

"What in the—?" Nan surged to her feet, as did her father and Rog. While she and Dad stood frozen with surprise, uncertain what to do, Rog dropped her hand and ran across the floor, toward the stairs and the chaos.

The shouts shifted beneath them, changing location as Mooch raced from the back of the store to the front and out onto the boardwalk. Rog changed directions too and ran down the front steps.

"Unlocked?" he yelled.

"From the inside, yes," she yelled back, her paralysis broken. She rushed to the stairs just in time to see Rog throw the door open.

She raced down so fast, she wasn't certain her feet hit all the treads. She burst onto the boardwalk and did a quick shuffle as she dodged around the couple who just missed getting knocked flat when she threw open the door. Off to the right, Mooch chased a kid in a black T-shirt.

The kid was running for all he was worth. Nan expected him to run down the first street ramp he came to, but no. He was running on a gradual angle across the boardwalk toward the beach. Mooch was right behind him with Rog a close third.

She chased after them. Way too soon, she began gasping for air through her mouth. Apparently lugging stock around didn't help respiratory health, at least not enough to make her race-ready. Any minute now, the stitch in her side would strike.

"Stop right there!" Mooch weaved around people like a halfback on his way to the goal line. He did his own version of a quick shuffle to avoid a family of five, all eating chocolate and vanilla soft-serve ice cream cones. The little boys stared at Mooch wide-eyed, ice cream melting down their arms.

"You're under arrest!" Mooch yelled at the black-shirted kid, ruining the effect of the threat when he slowed for a moment as a curvaceous redhead with long legs grabbed his attention. He actually ran backwards for a couple of steps to keep her in view, his goofy grin in full bloom. When a guy who looked like a professional wrestler joined the redhead, Mooch made a face and returned to business.

"Mooch! Get back here!" Rog raced after his protégé, passing the redhead without a glance, Nan was glad to see. He was intent on his goal, which, she realized, was to keep Mooch from getting himself hurt. The kid was charming and funny and clever, but he was a danger to himself.

"Trip him! Trip him!" Mooch pointed at the runner. The boy glanced back over his shoulder and made a face as he saw Mooch with his long legs gaining on him in spite of the redhead.

The runner finally made it across the boardwalk a block beyond Present Perfect. He grabbed the railing and with a last quick check on Mooch, vaulted over it, disappearing into space and darkness.

Nan gave a little scream as she watched the boy jump. She

pictured him lying several feet down on the sand, legs broken, body bruised. She tried to run faster, which was foolish because if he were hurt, she didn't know how to help beyond calling 911.

First aid. She had to take a first aid class so she'd know what to do in the future. Maybe in the winter when the store was closed and she had nothing to do, she could find a class. Maybe the community college had one in Seaside.

Mooch ran to the rail and looked over.

"Don't jump!" she yelled as her imagination now had Mooch writhing in pain as he hit the unforgiving sand. "Please don't jump!" Her words were lost in the conversations of the many vacationers around her, several of whom had stopped to see why all these people were racing past.

Rog pulled up beside Mooch who turned, his disgusted expression telling its own tale. Nan knew there were no broken legs or bruised bodies down there. There was no kid. He'd probably disappeared into the darkness under the boardwalk and was long gone.

Rog climbed through the railing and stood on the narrow ledge. He looked right and left, searching, then jumped.

Nan's breath caught. This time, the broken legs and bruised body belonged to Rog, which was ridiculous. The man knew what he was doing. He'd been trained to manage dangerous situations, and this one was probably as un-dangerous as they came. She slowed to a walk for the last few yards to prove to herself that she wasn't worried about his ability to handle himself.

Mooch leaned over the rail and yelled something. His lack of concern eased any anxiety hidden deep in Nan's heart. After a few moments, Rog climbed up the nearest flight of beach stairs. His expression was one of resignation, which turned to surprise when he saw her.

"Is there anybody left minding the store?" he asked as she came to his side.

"Good question." And one she hadn't considered as she'd chased him down the boardwalk. She turned and saw Ingrid standing in Present Perfect's doorway, looking their way. Nan waved to show everything was okay. Ingrid waved back and went inside.

Mooch and Rog turned back toward Present Perfect together. Rog stopped and held out a hand to her. With a happy smile, she grabbed it.

Mooch was so high on adrenaline he couldn't walk. He danced, he spun, he gesticulated wildly. "Did you see that? I chased him and I scared him! Oh, yeah, baby, I scared him."

When he passed the ice cream boys, whose mother was kneeling in front of them trying to clean them up, he ruffled their hair and high-fived them. "You can grow up to chase bad guys too, little men. Oh, yeah, you can." He growled at them.

The boys laughed and growled back, but their mother looked less than pleased at the prospect of her babies racing after criminals.

"Sorry," Nan mouthed to her.

Rog gave Mooch a gentle elbow in the side to get his attention. "'You're under arrest?' Are you nuts? You can't yell that at people."

"It seemed a good idea at the time," Mooch defended. "It sounded authoritative. Scary." He made his growling sound again.

"What if he'd taken exception to being chased by someone he thought was a cop and turned with a gun in his hand?" Rog shook his head. "Then it would have been very scary. And how would I have ever explained to Lori if you'd been shot? Geez, Mooch!" He ran his hand through his hair.

Mooch shrugged, not the least frightened by Rog's reprimand or aware that affection was the reason for his rebuke. "There was no gun, so it's a moot point. Besides, I told you I'm going to be a cop. I was just practicing." Mooch went into a fighter's crouch, punching the air. "I plan to fight for truth, justice, and the American way."

Rog raised his hands in surrender. "Okay, Superman. Just let me know when you learn to fly."

They reached Present Perfect and walked in to find

customers walking the aisles like nothing unusual had happened. Dad walked toward them, face wrinkled with concern. Nan had forgotten about him in her anxiety for Rog. Before Dad reached them, she squeezed Rog's hand.

"I'm sorry he got away," she whispered, "but you're okay, and that's what counts." She blushed. She sounded like a tween groupie gushing over her favorite boy band, but she meant every word.

He smiled at her. "You didn't have to worry. I was never in danger."

"I know, but I'm still glad."

His smile deepened, crinkling his eyes and making her heart beat faster. Her skin grew hot. Suddenly the atmosphere carried enough electrical charge to make her hair curl. She could practically feel her blood fizzing through her veins as they stared at each other.

CHAPTER SEVENTEEN

Mooch coughed. "In case you're interested, I'm okay too."

Nan blinked and came back to the world around her. She felt the blood rush to her face as she realized her father had seen that moment between her and Rog.

She told me you've taken up with someone unsatisfactory down here.

They didn't come more satisfactory than Rog, and she hoped Dad realized it and told Mom. She didn't want to fight them about Rog as she had about Present Perfect.

She turned to Mooch. "I'm so glad you're okay, too. After all, you're the hero here. You're the one who chased that kid, and at great potential risk to yourself."

Mooch stood straighter, and his eyes skewed to Tammy, handling a customer at the register. She kept writing information for the woman, looking up frequently with an anxious expression. She was missing all the excitement, having returned to her job like the good kid she was.

Nan decided to make a fuss over Mooch for Tammy's benefit. She went up on her tiptoes and kissed him on the cheek. "That's for risking everything for Present Perfect."

Two customers who had seen at least some of the action patted Mooch on the back, and Ingrid gave him a big hug, earning a frown from Tammy. Nan bit back a smile.

She turned to speak to her father, but he was no longer paying attention to her. He was looking around the store with a frown, studying, evaluating. She swallowed hard.

"It's a great store, Nan," Rog whispered in her ear. "He's bound to be impressed, and I think he might actually admit it."

As opposed to Mom, who wouldn't under any circumstances.

She watched Dad pick up a sand sculpture and turn the jar this way and that, examining it as if it were fine art. He put it down and ran a finger over a silver frame. His face gave away nothing.

Nan had to stop watching him for reactions, or she'd make herself a nervous wreck. She'd already done that this morning with her mother, and once a day was more than enough.

"Come on back to the office, Mooch, and tell me exactly what that kid did." She led the way to the back of the store. She was aware of Mooch picking up a vase on the way.

He slowed as he passed the register and Tammy. In what he must have thought was a whisper but was loud enough for the whole store to hear, he leaned toward Tammy and hissed, "Later, pretty lady."

Knowing full well he wasn't talking to her, Nan turned and gave him a huge smile. "Why, thank you, Mooch. We ladies do love to be called pretty."

Mooch stared at her, nonplussed. "Uh, you're welcome." He swallowed, then smiled broadly as if he'd been talking to her all along. Both Tammy and Rog laughed. So did Tammy's customer.

Shaking her head at the kid's chutzpah, Nan entered the office. Mooch followed and held out a beautiful vase. It was a little over a foot tall, white with stylized butterflies and blue flowers painted on it. "This is what that guy left."

Nan studied the vase, tracing the butterflies. She turned it upside down. "Wedgwood."

Dad had followed Nan, Mooch, and Rog into the office. "Are you saying he left something? He didn't try to take anything?"

"He always leaves something. This time it's that vase," Mooch said.

"So you weren't chasing a thief?"

Mooch frowned, seeing his reputation as a superhero crumbling. "He's trickier than any mere thief. He strikes any time, day or night, without regard to his personal danger or the danger to others in the vicinity."

Dad just looked at him.

Mooch flushed. "Maybe that's a bit of an overstatement."

"See that shelf of stuff?" Nan pointed. "That kid—or someone he's working for—left all those items. I don't know what to do with them, and it's driving me nuts!"

Dad studied the things on the shelf. "Strange indeed." He picked up the Winston Churchill Toby mug. "I like this."

"It's yours—if I ever find out where it came from and feel free to give it away." Or sell. Well, not the mug if Dad liked it, but the other things. Wouldn't that extra money feel good padding the store's finances, helping make up for the thin cash receipts?

The door to the storeroom flew open, and Aunt Bunny rushed in. Her wild red hair was iridescent in the overhead lighting, but her red bag was missing from her shoulder, a sure sign she had come in a hurry. "I heard you had a bit of excitement here."

Nan was amazed at the speed of information. "Where did you hear that?"

"Didn't hear. Saw. People have pictures on their phones. And videos. It was all over the Buc. It's probably all over the Internet. Wouldn't be surprised if it's on the nightly news." She pointed a finger at Mooch. "I recognized you, young man, chasing after that kid like some superhero. I'll have to make you an outfit. Do you want your cape to be red or black?"

Mooch actually blushed.

"Did you recognize him?" She looked at Rog and Nan. "Could you pick him out of a lineup?"

"I'll handle the questioning, Mrs. Truscott." Rog leaned against the desk. "Though I have to say, I'd hoped the leavery was over now that I'm here."

"I sort of hope not." Mooch was pacing the office, still high on excitement.

"Bite your tongue," Nan ordered as she put the vase on the shelf with the other things.

Mooch shrugged. "I think it's all great fun. And I want to

solve the mystery."

Aunt Bunny looked thoughtful. "Maybe that young man you chased didn't realize the police were on the case."

"You mean the person who sent him didn't tell him?" Rog frowned at the thought.

"You really think it's over?" Nan wanted it to be over. She needed it to be over. She pressed her hands together in an attitude of prayer. "Please let it be over."

Aunt Bunny rested her hand over her heart. "I bet it doesn't happen again."

"I hope you're right, Mrs. Truscott." Rog folded his arms over his chest. "I hope you're right."

"Boy, would I love to see those videos." Mooch bounced with excitement. "I want to see what the pursuit of truth, justice, and the American way looks like, especially with me as the pursuer."

"I'd like to see the videos, too," Rog said. "I need to find that kid and talk to him."

"Really?" Mooch's eyes sparkled with excitement. "We're going to the Buc?"

"Sure. You're the star of the show, and people will want to show you the pictures they took of you."

"Maybe ask for autographs," Aunt Bunny added.

"Yeah, I'm the star, and they might." His chest swelled about three sizes. "I'll be famous for my fifteen minutes while you walk around all cop-like, saying, 'Who has pictures of that handsome kid chasing the other kid?'"

Aunt Bunny pulled open the office door and pointed. "Go get 'em, young man."

Mooch looked at Nan. His yearning to go with Rog poured off him like water from an overflowing tub.

Nan patted his hand. "I think it's more important you help Rog than that you keep working here tonight. You can catch up tomorrow."

Mooch's smile could have lit Philadelphia. "Hey, Rog, will we have time to ride the End of the World?"

Rog blanched at the mention of the wild ride, making Nan

laugh.

"Go, guys." She shooed them toward the door. "Find the kid and solve my mystery."

"Yes, ma'am!" Mooch all but ran from the office, Rog following. At the door, Rog turned and gave Nan a slow wink that made her feel all warm and soft inside. She stood, staring at the spot where he'd been.

Aunt Bunny gave her a knowing look. "I told you he was the perfect one for you."

Nan bit back a smile. "As you might say, push posh. I've got to get back to the store."

"Deny it all you want, but I'm right. And now I want to talk to Stan, my favorite friend's favorite nephew."

Nan watched as Dad swept Aunt Bunny into a warm hug. "So good to see you, Bunny. How are you doing?"

She left them to talk, returning to the store where Tammy and Ingrid had everything well in hand. Using her tablet, Nan called up the Wedgwood site and found the vase. Butterfly Bloom priced at $725. She swallowed hard.

"It's beautiful," Ingrid whispered as she looked at the picture on the screen. "If it were mine, I'd never give it away."

Nan nodded. "Just shows you're a smart girl."

Ingrid flushed with pleasure.

Aunt Bunny and Dad walked out of the office. Aunt Bunny swept an arm out to indicate the store. "So how do you like your girl's inheritance?"

Dad glanced at Nan, who, though fiddling with the items Mooch had rearranged, was listening intently. "She loves it, doesn't she?"

"She does, and she's going to do very well."

Dad sighed. "It's so easy to think you know what's right for your kid."

"Tell me about it."

"How is Alana?"

Aunt Bunny's eyes skittered to Nan, who was now openly eavesdropping. "Ask your daughter. She can speak the truth better than I can. After all, I'm her mother and shouldn't say what I think."

"That bad?"

Aunt Bunny shrugged. "You know how she is."

Dad nodded as if he knew all too well.

Aunt Bunny studied him. "Did Elise send you down here to check on Nan? It was an unnecessary trip, you know. Rog is a wonderful guy."

"I'm getting that idea."

Aunt Bunny put a hand on Dad's arm. "You can relax, Stan. Our girl is doing fine. And I must leave. I've got to check on Rog and Mooch at the Buc." With a wave, she was gone.

Nan and Dad looked at each other across one of the counters. Nan's heart raced and her mouth was dry. If only she knew what he was thinking.

"This has been a very informative trip." Dad gave Nan a crooked smile and nodded as though deciding something positive. "I'm glad I came."

She felt a welling of love for him. "I'm glad too, Dad."

"Your store is very nice, and if it makes you happy, it makes me happy."

She rushed to hug him. "Thank you! You don't know what that means."

"Just so you know, Elise will not give you any more trouble about Brandon or the party." He kissed her cheek. "And that young man of yours seems most suitable."

"Oh, Dad, he is, though I'm not sure he's mine yet."

"But there's hope?"

She grinned. "There's hope." And that was the truth.

When he left, Nan checked her watch. Almost closing time. She went into the office intending to do some work. Instead she found herself studying the vase with the butterflies. It was a far cry from any vases she owned. Hers were ones left after a floral arrangement gift had died. Most were thanks to Tyler.

At closing time, Tammy and Ingrid came in. "Good night, Nan. See you tomorrow."

Nan waved a hand vaguely in their direction. "Make sure the front door is locked before you go."

"Already done," Tammy said. The girls left through the back door, and Nan was alone. She walked through the darkened store and double-checked the lock on the front door. She looked around, trying to decide where she'd put her register if she moved it as Rog suggested.

And where was he? Had he and Mooch learned anything at the Buc?

She slammed home the bolt on the back door and went upstairs. She sighed when she saw the tarp-shrouded bedroom. She pulled back one of the canvas drop cloths to uncover the bed. She wrestled one of the night tables back into place. When she set the lamp on top and flicked it on, Lizzie jumped onto her pillow.

"Hey, pretty lady." Nan reached out to pet the cat. No purr at the touch, but the cat didn't pull away. Nan couldn't help smiling. "Wait here. I've got a treat for you."

She rushed to the kitchen, checking Lizzie's water bowl as she passed. Still full. She grabbed several soft treats from the pouch and hurried back to the bedroom to catch Lizzie while she was still in a good mood. As the cat ate daintily from Nan's outstretched hand, there was no purr, but again, there was no pulling away.

Small steps.

CHAPTER EIGHTEEN

Rog and Mooch looked at several pictures and videos of the chase on the boardwalk. Mooch was much taken with the fact that his exploits were worthy of being captured by strangers. He especially liked the video with the beautiful redhead in it.

"She is sweet!" He patted his heart as he paused the video to study her.

Rog gave him a raised eyebrow. "I thought Tammy held your heart."

"Well, yeah, but a man can still appreciate beauty wherever he sees it."

"How about the kid you chased? Look familiar?"

"Since I've only been in Seaside a little more than a day, I can truthfully say I never saw him before."

"You're sure? You never saw him in the store?"

"Never saw him." His eyes lit. "But I bet I could pick him out of a lineup."

Rog had to laugh. "I don't think we're taking a lineup. We aren't even talking a crime."

Mooch looked thoughtful. "We aren't, are we? Oh, well. Can we ride the End of the World now?"

Glad Mooch's short attention span wasn't crucial to a real case, Rog said, "You can. Not me."

"Wimp."

"Definitely where that ride's concerned."

Rog sat on a bench on the boardwalk and pondered broken promises while Mooch rode the End of the World three times. He wasn't surprised when his phone rang.

"I gave that vase to him three days ago. I didn't realize he hadn't left it yet."

"So you mean to keep your word? There will be no more leavery?"

"No more. I promise."

"What about your confession?"

"It's coming."

"When?"

"Soon."

Rog said nothing, letting his silence communicate his unhappiness.

"I want to remind you that I haven't committed a crime."

He sighed. "She deserves to know."

"She does and she will. Trust me, Rog. I have a good reason for delaying my confession."

He disconnected as Mooch came loping across the boardwalk, his goofy grin creasing his face. "So cool! So cool! You should have gone with me."

Rog didn't bother to argue. "Let's go home."

He decided not to call Nan when he left the Buc. He had no news to give her, so he told himself he had no reason to call. It wasn't like they were a couple or anything, despite what she kept telling her parents. She was just a woman he was concerned about, just as he'd be for any other woman he met in the line of duty.

Liar, liar, pants on fire.

While it was true he had nothing to tell her about the leavery, the real reason he didn't call was because he was feeling antsy about their burgeoning friendship. Too much, too soon. He should never have volunteered to paint for her, but those hazel eyes had enticed him. When he came back tomorrow evening, he'd be cool, all reserved and remote, so she'd get over any ideas of being in a relationship. There would be no status change on Facebook.

It was late morning the next day when he stopped at Present Perfect. He wasn't coming to see Nan. He needed to learn if there was any more leavery, if Aunt Bunny had kept her word. At least, that was what he told himself.

Nan's eyes lit up when he walked in, and his stomach turned over with both distress and delight. When he was with her, it seemed perfectly normal that their friendship should progress at the speed of light. It was when they were apart that he wondered.

 She hurried toward him. "Did you find out anything last night? I've been going crazy wondering."

"Not really." He should have called when he left the Buc. It would have been the polite thing to do.

Her face fell, and he felt like he had failed her. He scanned the counters. "Did you find anything in the store today?"

She shook her head. "But the day is young yet."

He looked over her head and saw only one shopper. "Slow day?"

"No more than usual."

"A week from Friday starts the Fourth weekend."

"That'll be my test. It makes me nervous."

"Don't worry. You'll do fine."

"From your mouth to God's ears."

They smiled at each other, and he felt the same sensation of falling that he'd felt last night when they'd had that strange staring moment. He blinked himself out of the trance. It was definitely time to leave, to get far from her and the weird magic she exerted.

"How'd you like a coffee?" He blinked again, surprised at himself, and almost looked over his shoulder to see who had spoken. Instead, he tilted his head toward Ed's. "I was thinking a sticky bun too."

"It'll ruin your lunch."

"I'll make it my lunch. Want one?"

She grinned as if he'd offered her the moon. "I'd love one."

He walked to Ed's with her smile in his mind. Why was he fighting his attraction so hard? What was he scared of? A cute little brunette? Maybe it was leftover angst from Lori, not that she held any interest for him any longer. It was the idea of being dumped again, of living that ache again, of not being good enough again.

Ed smiled at him as he entered. "That was some footrace last night."

"Two coffees and two buns. You saw?"

"Hard not to. 'You're under arrest! Trip him! Trip him!'"

"That was not me."

"Of course not." Ed was enjoying himself.

"I usually go with, 'Stop! Police!'"

"Much more professional. Just like it's professional to come back and check on the crime victim this morning." Ed was reaching into his display case for the sticky buns, so Rog couldn't see his face, but he heard the teasing in his voice.

"A cop's gotta do what a cop's gotta do."

Ed straightened and held out a bag with the pastries. "Especially when the victim of the crime is such a lovely little thing."

Rog almost told Ed that there hadn't been a crime, but the thought of explaining leavery gave him a headache. He handed over a twenty. "Was her aunt as tiny as she is?"

Ed shrugged as he made change. "She wasn't tall, I can tell you that. You forgot she was so little because she had presence, you know? Char was a great lady. A great neighbor. When she died, I was afraid the property would go to Alana, but no. It went to Little Miss Cutie instead."

Rog frowned. "Why would it go to Alana?"

"Char and Bunny were tight. Real tight. Maybe Char saw Alana as her daughter by extension, you know? If Alana had gotten the store, then I'd be the only holdout on the block."

"Alana owns this whole block of stores?" Rog was floored.

"Except for Present Perfect and me. And I'm not selling. I figure I've got ten, fifteen more years here. My kids don't show any interest in the shop. They don't like baking, and the hours are terrible. Of course, those terrible hours put them all through college. When I go, they'll sell if I haven't already cashed in to pay for my retirement. Alana and Jason are offering top dollar."

"Jason?"

"Her real estate mogul husband."

"What do Alana and her husband plan to do with the properties?"

"Don't know. Could be something as simple as collect rents like they're doing now. Or maybe they plan to get the block rezoned and put in oceanfront condos, though I can't imagine the town authorities allowing that. More likely, they plan to bring in swanky chain stores and kick out all the little independents."

"You think the big names would come for such a short season?"

"I don't know. All I know is I'm not selling. I'm not helping Alana one-up her mom. I like Bunny too much."

"What do you mean, one-up?"

"Bunny and Joe own the block of businesses next to the Buc and several properties downtown." He stopped. "Well, I guess Bunny owns it all now. I think Alana and Jason have visions of doing at least as well as her parents. Whatever they're thinking, it just makes Alana driven and grumpy. Everybody liked Joe, and you know Bunny. What's not to like? Alana and Jason—not so much. Sad."

Coffee and treats in hand, Rog walked back to Present Perfect. No wonder Alana was hostile to Nan. She stood in the way of her plans. Ed's theory about Alana's need to be better than her parents offered one possible explanation for her hostility to her mother. Ed was right about one thing. Sad.

As he walked through the store to the office, Tammy stood behind the register handling a sale. He cocked an eyebrow at her. "Anything new?"

She shook her head no. No leavery. She gave him what she probably thought was a seductive smile, but Rog took care to keep his face expressionless. She should smile like that at Mooch and make his day.

When Rog left Present Perfect fifteen minutes later, he told himself he wasn't coming back until dinner and painting. When he stopped in at two in the afternoon, he admitted defeat. Nan was a magnet, and he was metal shavings pulled to her in spite of himself.

Of course, dinner exerted a strong pull a few hours later, and for the second night, it was delicious, a beef stew with warm from-the-oven cinnamon coffee cake to go with it.

"Did you see Aunt Bunny today?" Had she kept her promise?

"I didn't." She took his empty plate and walked to the stove.

"Phone call from her?"

"Nope. No Aunt Bunny and no leavery." She ladled more stew onto his plate.

"Huh." What was Bunny's game here? She'd promised.

"More coffee cake?" She smiled at him and cut a large piece.

It had only been two days since Bunny gave her word, but it felt like longer. Day One, Nan's parents had showed up both times Bunny came to the store. No privacy for a conversation. Today, Day Two, she hadn't come visiting at all. He sighed. What was she waiting for?

He was finishing his meal when he brought up Alana.

"Did you know she owns most of the stores in your block?"

Nan shook her head.

"According to Ed, she wants to buy you out."

Nan looked thoughtful, got up from her seat, and rooted around in her trash can under the sink. Lizzie jumped up on the counter and watched with great interest.

"Yes!" Nan waved a flyer in the air, and Lizzie batted at it with one black paw.

"Sorry, pretty girl, not for you." Nan gave the cat a scratch under the chin. Lizzie didn't look impressed, but she lifted her head so Nan had a better angle.

Nan came to the table and held the flyer out to him.

A & J Mulrooney: local independent realtors working hard for you.

The picture of the smiling woman didn't look much like the angry Alana Rog had seen.

"So the A is Alana," Nan said. "And the J?"

"Her husband Jason." He helped himself to a third piece of coffee cake.

"I get letters from A & J Mulrooney all the time, but I don't even open them. I read the first one, which was an offer for the store. Since I wasn't interested in selling, I tossed it and all the others."

"Ed says you and he are the only properties on the block that Alana and her husband don't own."

Nan cut a sliver of coffee cake so thin Rog was afraid it would crumble before she got it to her mouth. "Alana called a couple of times back when I first got the property. She was all friendly and charming until I told her I wasn't interested in selling. Then the crabby Alana appeared." She blinked as Lizzie jumped into her lap. "I didn't realize A & J Mulrooney was Alana's real estate firm, probably because the name Mulrooney didn't mean anything to me."

When Nan started clearing the table, Rog took his dishes to the sink, where he rinsed them and stuck them in the dishwasher. It was the least he could do after the wonderful meal.

Nan leaned against the counter. "You don't think Alana's desire to buy me out has anything to do with the leavery, do you?"

"Interesting question." Rog leaned against the counter beside her, letting their shoulders bump. "I doubt it, but I'll think on it."

Nan gave him a bump back. "You do that."

They grinned at each other, and what started as a simple meeting of the eyes turned into another of those vertigo-inducing moments. He wasn't sure who blinked first, but Nan cleared her throat. "I've got to get back to work."

Rog straightened. "Yeah. Sure. Me too."

The sound of her footfalls faded before he took a step.

Nan sent Mooch up to help him move the rest of the furniture away from the walls, and Rog spent the evening taping off the windows and baseboards and cutting in around them, into the corners, and along the ceiling. The can said the paint had primer in it and you could save yourself a step. This pink would be a bear to cover, so he hoped the claim was true.

He listened to music as he painted, relaxed and at peace. Nothing terrible had happened on the job today, and he'd had a wonderful dinner. He was doing a task he found soothing, and there was a very pretty lady downstairs.

Good day, Lord. A very good day.

He finished dealing with the corner behind the huge chest of drawers, feathering the paint at the edges of his strokes so it would blend with the paint from the roller when he did the walls. He wrote a big ROG on the facing wall before he knelt to paint along the baseboard. The signature would be covered when he did the walls and no one but he would know it was there. Well, maybe Nan would notice. But he would know. He wasn't like one of the Grand Masters signing a work of art, but his work was marked.

He lowered to his knees, setting his paint, which was poured into an old Cool Whip container, on the floor in front of him. He liked working with the smaller container rather than the larger, heavier can.

Suddenly, Nan came around the chest with a drink she'd gotten for him at Ed's Eats, or so the green ED'S on the yellow cup indicated. He hadn't heard her coming because of his earbuds. She just appeared, holding out the beverage to him.

"For you."

At least that's what he thought she said. He pulled out his earbuds and reached for the glass. "Thanks. I was getting thirsty."

Nan stepped forward to hand the cup to him—and put her foot right in the paint container. She gave a little yelp as she felt the container tilt and the paint slide into her sandal. "Oh, no!"

She stepped back, lifted a hand to steady herself against the wall, and hit dead center on the ROG. Her hand slid on the still-wet paint, and she half-fell into the corner and its wet paint. She pushed herself upright, trying to steady herself on one foot.

Instinctively, she shook her wet foot. Paint flew. The chest became more speckled than a wren's egg. So did Rog, who was having a hard time standing in the little space behind the chest without stepping in the paint. He finally staggered to his feet, brush in hand, and reached for her before she stepped in the paint again. It was flowing with amazing quickness right toward her other foot, the one she was standing on. She reached for him to steady herself and grabbed the paintbrush for her trouble.

"Ee-uw!" She shoved the brush away and started to tilt again. She flailed and hopped and hit the wall with her back. She hung there, suspended like a human Tower of Pisa. The tarp beneath her foot shifted under the sharp angle of pressure, and she started to slide down the wall.

If she hit the floor, she'd be sitting in paint.

Rog caught her upper arms and hauled her upright. She grabbed him at the waist. They stood, she blinking up at him, he gazing down at her. Magnet and metal shavings.

He swallowed. "You okay?"

"Sure." She looked him up and down. "You're spattered. I spattered you."

He glanced down at himself. He was spattered, all right. "It's water-based. It'll wash off, though I'm not too sure about your sandal." He pointed. "Sandals." The paint surrounded her second foot, and it was closing in on him.

He moved quickly, sliding an arm across her back and one under her knees and lifting her up. She gave a small squeak of surprise and threw her arms around his neck to steady herself. He took a giant step to avoid the gray-green lake and carried her into the bathroom, paint dripping from her feet as they went. He set her down in the tub and steadied her with his hands on her waist. Such a tiny waist!

He let go reluctantly. "I've got to go back and get that paint cleaned up before it runs under the tarp and ruins your rug."

She stared down at her gray-green feet. "Sure. I'll just rinse myself off." She ran a hand through her hair. "I feel like such an idiot!"

He grinned. "But you saved the lemonade." He pointed to the cup still in her other hand, lid tightly in place.

She stared at the yellow cup, then at him. "Priorities." She held it out to him.

He took it. "But where's the straw?"

CHAPTER NINETEEN

When Nan climbed the stairs after ten that night, she was running on empty. She walked to the bedroom door and peered in.

"You in there?" She leaned wearily against the door jamb so it could hold her up as she waited for Rog's response. After the paint fiasco, there was no way she was going to enter the room, even if she'd had the energy to walk that far. Queen Elizabeth came and sat beside her, head cocked as if waiting for the answer too.

"Over here." His hand shot up behind the bureau. "Just have to do from here to the corner and I'm finished."

He sounded full of life, and she managed a mental snarl at such vitality. He made her feel more tired than she already was. She'd spent a frustrating two hours trying to reconcile delivery slips with sales records and inventory, all without success. At least there'd been a bit more cash in the till today.

She sighed and forced herself to be gracious, because he deserved her appreciation. The soothing gray-green lining the ceiling, the windows, the corners, and the baseboards already eased her stress in a way the pink could never do.

To show her appreciation, she made herself ask, "Want a bowl of ice cream when you're finished?" Surely she could find the strength to scoop some rocky road into a bowl.

"Know what I want?" His voice was muffled. Or was she so tired she no longer heard clearly? "I want to go for a walk."

What? "Nice. Have fun." She pushed off the jamb and went to one of her chairs in front of the window. She sank into it and spun to face the dark. From up here when you sat, you looked right out to the beach, missing the boardwalk entirely unless you leaned forward. She looked out at the dark beach and black ocean beyond, laid her head back, and closed her eyes.

A hand on her shoulder caused her to jerk awake with a little yelp.

"Sorry." He smiled. "I didn't mean to scare you."

She bit back a yawn. "Not to worry. I don't scare easily."

His smile broadened. "If you say so."

"I don't. I was just a little startled. That's all."

He reached out to her. "Let's go."

She stared groggily at his extended hand. "What?"

He crooked his fingers. "Come take a short walk with me. You've been inside all day, and I've been breathing paint fumes. We need the fresh air."

What she needed was her bed and a good night's sleep. What she said was, "Sure, a short walk. Sounds good."

She grabbed his hand and let him pull her to her feet. She grabbed her fleece jacket, a barrier against the damp chill she knew would have crept into the sea air. She followed Rog down the front stairs, stifling a yawn as she went. They stepped onto the boardwalk, now quiet and mostly empty since the shops and food places were closed for the night.

They turned away from the Buc, which still lit up the night in the distance, and walked into the quiet and dark. With the moon barely a crescent, the beach and the ocean were invisible on their left, though the low rumble of the waves reached them. With no one in front of them, they could have been alone in the world as they moved through the pools of light cast by the street lamps lining the boardwalk.

For a while, they walked without talking, their silence companionable, comfortable. Even when Rog took her hand, all they did was smile at each other. When she shivered, he dropped her hand and wrapped his arm around her. She was happy to snuggle against his side. She resisted the urge to rest her head on his shoulder.

A cry sounded from the beach, and she startled. All the tales she'd ever heard of trouble on lonely stretches of night-shrouded sand slid through her mind. "What was that?"

Rog's arm fell away, all his attention focused on the possible trouble. "Stay here. I'll be back." He loped to the closest stairs to the beach and threw her an absent-minded wave as he disappeared down the steps.

Nan leaned against the rail, squinting into the night as she tried her best to make out Rog's dark shadow against the black of the beach and ocean. He seemed headed toward a small light bobbing in the darkness. From here, she couldn't tell if it was in the water or on the beach.

Footsteps sounded behind her, and her heart tripped. She spun to see a couple hurrying past without a glance her way. The man said something low, and the woman turned to him, her teeth flashing white as she smiled at him.

Feeling foolish at her accelerated heart rate, Nan watched the couple for a few seconds. When their arms snaked around each other's waists, she smiled. Romance was in the air.

She turned back to the beach, looking again for Rog, but all she saw was black. The light that pooled around her from the street lamp made the space outside its reach even darker. The itchy feeling of being alone and exposed rippled through her.

Footsteps pounded, approaching from the rear. She spun again and tensed as a pair of teenaged boys ran up the ramp from the street and hurried her way, only to run past. She heard one say, "End of the World." She glanced at her watch. They had fifteen minutes before the Buc went silent for the night.

She laughed at herself and her jumpiness, but the itchiness increased. "Come on, Rog," she muttered. "Get back here."

A pair of nighttime joggers shook the boards as they passed, and a man with a very large dog—a Newfoundland maybe?—surged up the ramp. Too bad she didn't have a big animal like that at her side. She wouldn't feel as vulnerable and alone.

The man with the dog sneezed, and she jumped. He

sneezed again, pulled out a handkerchief, and blew his nose. The big dog waited patiently, looking at Nan with interest. He gave a deep combination bark and growl.

The dog's interest drew the man's attention to her. "Hello. Dark tonight, isn't it?"

She gave a little smile and watched the dog pull on his lead, anxious to get to her.

Okay, she'd had enough. She'd never considered herself a Nervous Nellie, but she felt like one now. She pushed off the railing and headed for the steps to the beach. The dog barked at her again as she hurried down.

She hit the beach running and headed straight for the small moving light. She looked over her shoulder, half expecting the man and the dog to be on her tail. No one was there.

Still.

Now the beach, dark and strange, made her skin prickle. She picked up speed. She needed Rog. She felt relief as she was able to make out shapes moving in the little light.

"Rog?" There was no answer, but she thought her voice was probably lost in the noise of the waves. She called louder. "Rog!"

One of the black figures turned, his face in shadows cast by the light behind him. "Nan?"

She ran the last few feet to him, pointing back to the boardwalk. "Too weird up there alone."

"So you don't scare easily, huh?"

She heard the teasing tone and made a face. "I don't. I just felt lonely."

"If you say so."

Another dark figure rushed toward her, and she automatically took a step back.

Rog reached for her. "It's okay."

She grabbed his hand. "It is?"

"Hey, boss! Imagine seeing you here."

She blinked. "Mooch?"

"Yeah, it's me." He sounded excited and pleased with life.

"That cry we heard?" Rog pulled her in front of him and

rested his hands on her shoulders.

"Mooch?" Not hard to guess.

"That's because Clooney gave me a present." Mooch pointed at the little light, and Nan realized a man was wearing a band about his head with a bulb in the front. "You met Clooney yet? Clooney, this is my boss, Nan. She owns Present Perfect."

"Ah, Char Patterson's niece." Clooney's voice seemed to come from the air, since she couldn't see anything but his light.

"You knew my aunt?" Nan couldn't even make out his shadow behind the brightness.

"Wonderful woman. I'm very sorry for your loss."

Nan knew she was truly tired when she felt tears gather at the man's kindness. She willed them away but still had to clear her throat. "Thank you."

Clooney gave a laugh. "It was the strangest thing. She always used to tell me about God."

Nan recognized that baffled tone of voice. She used to sound the same way when talking about Char. "Oh, yeah. I remember that well."

"You become a believer?" Clooney sounded genuinely interested in the answer.

"I did. You?" If he could ask her, she could ask him.

"Not quite there yet, but I'm getting closer every day."

"Clooney's using a metal detector to find stuff in the sand." Mooch spoke, and Nan knew from the excitement in his voice that the adventure of finding stuff captivated him.

"Look. He gave me these." Mooch held out a pair of glasses in metal frames, much the worse for having been buried in the sand.

"Ah." Nan wasn't sure what she was supposed to say about ruined glasses.

"Clooney gives stuff to lots of people." Mooch looked at the man to be sure he had it right. "Stuff that means something."

"Right." She couldn't imagine what the glasses might mean.

"I gave Mooch the glasses because he's looking for his

future." Clooney's voice held laughter as if he realized Nan's skepticism. "To find it, he has to look through the right lens."

Nan peered at the glasses again as the beam of Clooney's headlamp fell directly on them. "I'm afraid these won't be much help."

"They're a metaphor," Mooch said, as if Nan were foolish for not realizing it.

Nan blinked. "A metaphor?" She could feel a surprise that matched hers pouring from Rog.

"Hey, I listened in English." He sounded offended at her surprise. "A metaphor is when one thing stands for another. The road was a ribbon. Like that."

Nan grinned at him. He was only about ten years her junior, but she felt like his mom, all proud and pleased. "Good man, Mooch."

"Believe me, I'm impressed." Rog gave the boy a gentle punch on the arm, then turned to Nan. "I was just saying I thought the best lens for him to look through might be prayer."

"Yeah." Mooch didn't sound too enthusiastic about the idea. "Like prayer will show me what to do."

"It just might." Nan pointed in the general direction of home. "Prayer gave me Present Perfect."

"Interesting," Clooney said. "I was just telling Mooch that I'm realizing the benefits of prayer more all the time. I'm a late learner. Mooch is lucky. He can be an early learner."

Mooch shrugged, noncommittal.

"The right lens, Mooch." Clooney looked down at his equipment, and the light from his headband fell on a state-of-the-art metal detector and a child's pail with a red beach spade sticking out of it. "I have to go. I want to cover five more blocks before calling it a night."

"Can I come along?" Mooch spun his glasses by one bow.

"It's getting late, Mooch." Rog took the glasses, studied them, and rubbed the lenses on his shirt.

"You can't rub out scratches." Mooch took them back and stuck them on his head like sunglasses worn inside. "The scratches add character."

Clooney clapped Mooch on the back. "This is a smart young man."

Mooch beamed.

Rog pointed a finger at the boy. "Half an hour. See if you can beat me home."

"I'll send him on his way." Clooney started down the beach.

With a grin and a little skip, Mooch followed. "Can I use the metal detector? I won't hurt it. I promise."

Nan glanced at Rog and smiled. He reached for her hand, and they started back in the direction of the store. Somehow, walking on the beach in the dark felt like the most romantic thing ever. She gave in to the urge to rest her head on his shoulder. She was feeling all romantic when he spoke.

"So do we have to go to that thing tomorrow night?" He did not sound enthusiastic.

Mood killer. She straightened. "I did it again, didn't I? Dragged you into something you knew nothing about."

"I'm getting used to it." Was that a smile she heard in his voice or just wishful thinking?

"I need to go," she said. "But you don't have to. And I won't hold it against you if you don't."

"But then you'd be going alone."

She heard a shell crack beneath her feet. "There are worse things."

"Tell me what time, and I'll arrive in my pumpkin carriage."

Relief washed through her. She did not want to go alone. "I'll be waiting in my glass slippers."

When he leaned over, it was so easy to turn her face to his.

His lips were soft, his chin scratchy, and his arms around her strong.

CHAPTER TWENTY

A quick trip to Seaside's lone bridal shop Thursday morning brought a chirpy saleswoman to Nan's side before the door had even closed behind her. She was not the smooth saleswoman in black seen on *Say Yes to the Dress*. From her fuchsia T-shirt that read in curving black script *Seaside Brides Are the Prettiest* to her rhinestone-encrusted flip-flops, she was a seashore woman.

"Oh, my dear," she sparkled, "you'll be such a lovely bride."

"Uh, I'm not the bride."

"Bridesmaid, then?"

Nan shook her head. "I need a dress for a formal event, but—" She hated saying she couldn't spend much. All her money had to go back into Present Perfect, so she had little to spare for a one-time event dress.

Some of the chirp disappeared as the saleswoman saw large commissions disappearing, but she understood what Nan didn't articulate. "Our sale room is over here."

She led the way to a little alcove where dresses were scrunched together on a rack. "Discontinued models and samples from this summer's line, which of course has now been replaced by next summer's dresses. Our brides are wonderful at planning ahead." Which Nan obviously was not.

The store's door opened to five women, obviously a bride and her friends, and the woman disappeared without a backward glance.

Nan studied the yards of colorful cloth pressed into one big fabric rainbow. How was she to find a single dress in this crush? At least things were arranged by size.

She pulled dresses free and examined them, stuffing them back as her desperation grew. What if she didn't find anything she liked? There was no way she could drive to her parents' house to recover a dress from the things stored there. She could just hear her mother.

"You can't come to my party, but you can come for a dress? Where are your priorities, Nanette?"

Well, when all else fails, pray. Right?

Dear Lord, I need a dress.

She knew He was probably not too happy with her for making believe things were more with Rog than they were, but she really did need a dress. *Please, Lord!*

And there it was, a silky soft sage green dress with a full, swirling skirt and a scoop neck that would sit at her collarbone. She had just the necklace of faux pearls and crystals in the store to finish it off.

She tried the dress on, turning and twirling in front of the three-way mirror, thrilled with the fit. She pulled her bone-colored T-straps out of her bag and slid them on. Not really the shoes the dress called for, but her strappy silver stilettos were at Mom and Dad's with her formals and she'd never quite gotten around to getting glass slippers.

"Ah, you found something," said the saleswoman. "I must say, it looks wonderful on you."

Nan would have appreciated the compliment more if the woman didn't sound so surprised.

Thursday night, she waited anxiously for Rog. She kept checking her reflection in the full-length mirror mounted on the back of the bedroom door. She thought of going down and asking Tammy and Ingrid how she looked but decided against it. It felt too tell-me-I'm-pretty.

Well, she felt pretty, and her heart fluttered at the thought of Rog's reaction. He'd mainly seen her in Present Perfect shirts and slacks. What would he think of her tonight?

She grinned as she recalled how she had been dreading this night. It was amazing what a lovely dress could do to one's outlook. Well, a lovely dress and an adorable man.

The back buzzer sounded. He was here. She hurried to the top of the stairs and

stopped. *Slow and easy, Nan. Slow and easy.* She was not a sixteen-year-old on a first date.

True, but Roger Smedley Eastman was waiting for her. She grinned and hurried downstairs. The peep camera showed him looking very handsome in a tux. What was it about a man in a tux? Nan's hand went to her rapidly beating heart.

She pulled the door open, and they stared at each other for a moment. Then Rog's mouth quirked up in a half smile.

"You look wonderful."

She grinned. "You look pretty good yourself." Adorable!

"Your dress matches your wall color."

She pretended offense. "That's the best you can do?"

He tried to look confused. "Well, it does."

"I was going more for a match to my eyes."

He gave her a sly, twinkling look. "Your eyes are too lovely to compare to anything as trivial as a dress, no matter how pretty."

She laughed, delighted.

He stepped inside and gave her a light kiss on the cheek. It was just a peck, but she was certain her heart stuttered. She kept looking at him, hoping for more, maybe a repeat of last night's.

"We've got company." Rog gave a head tilt toward the office door behind her. She spun and found Tammy, Ingrid, and Mooch crowded in the doorway.

Tammy rushed forward. "Oh, Nan, you look so pretty." She pulled out her phone. "Pictures!"

"But not in the office," Ingrid said. "We don't want clutter in the background. Outside."

They trooped out to the narrow boardwalk that ran behind the line of shops.

"Who's minding the store?" Nan asked.

"No one." Tammy waved a hand to shoo that tiny problem away. "We'll only be a moment."

Nan began, "Someone—"

"I'll go." Ingrid headed back inside. "But you both look great!"

"Okay, first just Nan," Tammy ordered. Obediently, Nan stood by the railing that edged the narrow boardwalk. As she smiled for the kids, she thought the parking lot and motel behind them were only a marginally better background than the office clutter.

"Now just Rog." Tammy motioned to him.

Nan moved aside, and Rog leaned casually against the rail.

Mooch pulled out a phone too, his expression all calculation. "More GQ, Rog. Hand in your pocket. I want a picture for Lori and the weasel."

Tammy narrowed her eyes. "Who's Lori?"

"His old girlfriend. I want to show her what she gave up." He took a couple of shots. "Oh, and she's my sister."

"No! Rog used to go with your sister?" Tammy looked appropriately scandalized.

"They were engaged, and Lori broke it off."

Rog looked at Nan and shook his head in bemusement. She smiled. Why any woman would let Rog get away was beyond her.

Tammy matched Mooch's conspiratorial grin. "Then we've got to show her her beautiful replacement."

In concert the two kids motioned Nan and Rog together.

"Stand close," Tammy ordered.

"Real close." Mooch smashed his hands together. "Put your hand on her waist, Rog."

Tammy nodded. "Stand a little behind her. Angle a bit. That's right. Now smile."

Cameras clicked and Nan smiled as she was told, but her attention was on the man beside her, his warm hand on her waist, his chest rising and falling against her back.

"Okay, guys." She hoped no one noticed her breathless voice. "You've got to get back to work, and we need to go."

Tammy and Mooch backed toward the propped-open shop door.

"Have fun, kids," Mooch called. "Don't forget your curfew."

"Yeah," Tammy agreed. "We wouldn't want to have to ground you for the next month."

Rog put gentle pressure on Nan's lower back to direct her toward the stairs to the parking lot. He laughed. "I feel like I'm on my way to the prom."

"It's their point of reference for fancy dress. Here, give me your arm. I have to walk on tiptoe so my heels don't catch between the boards."

~ * ~

"Table one?" Nan held out their place cards. "Surely not."

"You said your aunt was part of the committee."

"But I'm not. I can't sit there. We can't sit there."

"I don't think we have a choice." Rog took her hand and led her into the dining room filled with linen-covered round tables with elaborate floral arrangements in the center of each. Men in tuxes or dark suits stood in contrast to the women in a rainbow of summer colors. Servers in black offered trays of hors d'oeuvres and beverages.

Rog steered them toward the front of the room. As she went, Nan smiled at anyone who looked her way. People smiled politely back.

"That's the mayor." Rog pointed out a handsome man with silver hair and a matching mustache. "He used to be the owner of a large auto dealership. He retired here and used that sales experience in local politics. Those two men with him are commissioners, as is the lady in the blue dress. The man in the uniform is my boss, Chief Gordon."

At that moment Chief Gordon saw Rog and nodded. He raised his hand and gave a little flick of his fingers.

"Is it good or bad he wants you?" Nan asked. "Should you be in uniform, too?"

"I'm not here on business like he is."

There was a flurry of names and handshakes as Rog

introduced her to the chief and his companions.

"I know what Officer Eastman does." Chief Gordon turned to her in the lull following the introductions. "What about you, Miss Patterson?"

"I have a gift shop called Present Perfect located on the boardwalk."

"Oh." The woman commissioner was suddenly interested. "Char Patterson's place. You know, Chief. Next to Excellent Ed's." She laughed. "That's what my husband and I call Ed's Eats."

"Your aunt was a wonderful woman," Chief Gordon said. "It's a pleasure to meet you, Miss Patterson. I'll see you tomorrow, Eastman."

With that gentle dismissal, Nan took Rog's arm, and they continued their search for their table. Nan noted the elegant printed program sitting on each pewter charger.

Five people—an older couple, a middle-aged couple, and a young woman not too much younger than Nan—were already seated at the table, and Nan knew none of them. The older man with a Friar Tuck circle of white hair stood as did a sturdy redheaded woman in a deep blue gown that made her look classy in spite of her size.

The man held out his hand. "Pete Sterling. And this is my wife, Blossom Buchanan Sterling."

Blossom Buchanan Sterling grinned. "My given name's Patricia, but it's always been Blossom. I married Pete to get away from the Blossom Buchanan."

"The only reason," Pete said amiably.

"The only reason," Blossom agreed as she smiled at her husband. Pete kissed the top of her head.

The other man at the table stood and extended his hand.

"This is our nephew, Mike," Pete said, "and his wife Marge, and their daughter, the lovely Jodi."

Jodi blushed. "Thanks, Uncle Pete."

"Mike's a high school principal, Marge is a pharmacist, and Jodi is a graduate student working on her MBA." Pete looked at Mike and Marge. "Nan is Char's great-niece."

"Oh, Char was such a wonderful lady," Marge said. "I'm so sorry for your loss, and we're glad to have you here as her representative. I'm sure it will mean a lot to—"

A flurry of movement brought a woman in red rushing to the table. "Pete, Blossom, I can't find—"

The woman stopped and took a step back as she stared at Nan. Nan stared back. Alana?

"What are you doing here?" The hostility in Alana's voice was obvious, and Nan could hear the shocked intake of breath from both Blossom and Marge.

"Hello, Alana." She forced herself to smile, even if it was more a baring of teeth than a gracious curving of the lips. "Nice to see you. You remember Rog Eastman, of course."

Alana obviously didn't, but then she'd only seen him for a minute, and then he'd been in uniform.

"Mrs. Mulrooney," Rog said pleasantly.

Alana ignored him and turned to Pete and Blossom, "What's she doing here?"

Before either of them could answer, a familiar voice said, "She's my guest. I invited her."

CHAPTER TWENTY-ONE

Nan spun to see Aunt Bunny, only it was Aunt Bunny as she'd never seen her before. Her often flyaway red hair was carefully, beautifully styled, and her rag-tag clothes were replaced by a gorgeous white gown that shimmered when she moved. She wore diamonds in her ears and around her neck. She looked like a chic and wealthy woman instead of the poor old lady Nan knew and loved.

Nan felt her mouth hanging open and snapped it shut. She blurted, "Aunt Bunny, you look so pretty!"

"Surprising, isn't it?" Aunt Bunny smiled.

Nan flushed. "I didn't mean—"

"Sure you did. And you should. You're used to me in my summer-at-the-Buc persona."

Blossom laughed. "She can't wait until she can go to the Buc and let her hair down. For as long as I can remember, even when we were kids, Bunny lived for summer."

"And for being free!" Aunt Bunny spread her hands wide. "Joe and I were never happier than at the Buc."

Alana sniffed, and Aunt Bunny patted her hand. "I know, dear. Such a trial for you."

The man whose photograph Nan had seen in the real estate flyer joined the group and stood behind Alana.

"Hello, Jason." Aunt Bunny smiled at him.

He nodded to her. "Mother." The coolness in his tone made it clear he felt the same about Aunt Bunny as Alana did.

Aunt Bunny sighed, then turned and smiled at Rog. "Good to see you, Rog."

"Good to see you, Mrs. Truscott." He leaned down and kissed her on the cheek. Her face pinked with pleasure as she turned to Nan. "Remember what I said concerning you-know-who?" She tilted her head in Rog's direction.

Now it was Nan's face flaming. She could feel the heat. "Aunt Bunny!"

Aunt Bunny laughed. "I take it you've met my sister and her husband."

Nan looked from Aunt Bunny to Blossom. Now that she knew what she was looking for, she could see the resemblance. The facial structure with the high cheekbones and deep-set brown eyes. The sharp, all-seeing intelligence that radiated from both. Even the hair, probably helped by a salon given the women's ages, was a color that went with their skin and eyes. "We met them just now, but I didn't realize Blossom was your sister."

Blossom *Buchanan* Sterling. Nan felt the world tilt. Bunny *Buchanan* Truscott?

"Blossom and Bunny Buchanan." Aunt Bunny grinned. "It's a good thing our parents were great people, or those names would have been enough to cause a family rift. What was cute at three years old is a bit strange at seventy-five."

"I thought..." The words died on Nan's lips. She didn't know what to say. She had felt *sorry* for Aunt Bunny, who lived in the tacky little apartment beside the noisy Buc. She had thought her aunt's best friend couldn't afford better. She had thought Aunt Char was wonderful to be close to someone with so little when she herself was comfortably set. In fact, Aunt Bunny had probably been slumming when she hung out with Aunt Char.

Aunt Bunny had funded a hospital! Well, a hospital wing, but still. And probably Blossom and her husband had been in on it too.

Nan glanced down at the program resting in front of her and read the words in raised gold lettering —*Dedication of the Buchanan Children's Place*. The *Buchanan* Children's Place.

Of course it wasn't surprising that whoever owned the Buc

was wealthy. It was a gold mine, crowded every night with thousands of people happily spending lots of money. That the Buchanans would fund a hospital wing was a fine thing, a reasonable thing, but that Aunt Bunny was a Buchanan! Another thing all together.

Nan turned to Rog and realized he wasn't surprised. He'd known Aunt Bunny was a Buchanan. He had listened to her talking about poor Aunt Bunny and said nothing to correct her. Her world was seriously off-kilter, and he just smiled at her as if all was normal. Or was there concern lurking behind that smile? She frowned. "You knew." She indicated the room and the program with a wave of her hand.

He nodded.

"How long?"

"From the night we had dinner at her place."

She couldn't believe her ears. "And you didn't tell me?"

"She promised me she would tell you."

She stared at him, feeling betrayed. It was stupid to react so strongly—one part of her understood that. But he should have told her. Her chest felt tight, and she had to work to breathe. It was Tyler not telling her about Jennifer all over again.

Rog reached for her hand. "It's okay."

She stared at him a minute, clutching her hands tightly at her waist. No way was she holding his hand, all sweetheart-y and caring. He'd known and hadn't said a word.

She thought of her father talking so familiarly with Aunt Bunny the other night. Dad knew who Bunny was. Of course he did. After all, Aunt Char was his aunt, and Aunt Bunny was Char's best friend.

Nan was the only one in the dark, the only one not invited into the club. "Excuse me," she said to no one in particular. She did not wait for a response before she fled.

She weaved among the tables, trying to be polite to the people standing in her way, until she finally made it out of the ballroom and into the corridor. She scanned the space, spied the sign for the restroom, and pushed her way inside. There were others in the ladies' room, but Nan knew none of them.

She wanted to be alone, to process what she'd just learned. She waited her turn for a stall and sat, fully clothed, taking care her gown didn't touch the floor. She looked at the lovely sage fabric and thought of the money she'd spent. She thought of her excitement at spending the evening with Rog, so handsome in his tux. She thought of chic Aunt Bunny.

She wanted to cry.

Dear Lord, I feel so dumb. Maybe I'm overreacting, but I feel betrayed.

Well, maybe betrayed was too strong. Betraying was what spies did, or unfaithful spouses, or larcenous business partners. Okay, not betrayed. But foolish, definitely. Hurt, oh yeah.

Not that Aunt Bunny shouldn't be rich. It was a good thing that she could make decisions about retirement communities without worrying about whether she could afford one. But Nan had been deceived—that's what hurt so—deceived by everyone who mattered to her.

Gradually, the ladies' room emptied, and she was the only one left. She sighed. That meant the dinner was being served, and she was making a spectacle of herself by hiding.

A thought hit her. She had the power to ruin Aunt Bunny's big night. Well, maybe not ruin it—that might be overstating— but certainly to taint it. She could be frosty in her conversation, withdrawn in her demeanor, critical in her comments.

In short, she could be Alana.

She sat up straight. Never!

So Aunt Bunny had purposely misled her. To balance that fact, she knew Aunt Bunny liked her. And she liked Aunt Bunny. She didn't think the little old lady who lived next to the Buc was a phony, a character created just to mislead Nan. According to Blossom, that person was who Aunt Bunny was, at least partly. She was also a rich, elegant woman.

Nan stood and exited the stall. Enough behaving like a junior high girl. Chin up. Shoulders back.

She walked to the sink and washed her hands while she wondered what Aunt Bunny's off-season house was like. A mansion? Or just a big house with lots of land and people to tend it for her? How many bedrooms? Certainly more and bigger than the little apartment. Had some ritzy interior designer made it a museum of good taste, or did Aunt Bunny's carny side intrude?

Nan froze as she reached for a towel. Could it be? No. It couldn't. No, no, no!

Yes. Everything pointed to what had to be true.

Aunt Bunny was responsible for the leavery.

CHAPTER TWENTY-TWO

Nan's stomach cramped and her chest hurt. In slow motion, she dried her hands, then wrapped her arms about herself to hold in the pain.

Why? When Aunt Bunny knew how much it upset her, why had she continued?

The bathroom door opened, and Nan struggled to hide the hurt she knew had to show on her face. She didn't want some stranger worrying over her.

"We need to talk."

Nan knew that voice. She spun to face Aunt Bunny. "You did it! You knew how much it bothered me, and you still did it!"

Aunt Bunny studied the tile in the ladies' room floor for a minute. Then she raised her head and threw back her shoulders. "If you mean the leavery, yes, I did it, though I didn't realize how upset you were until you called the cops. Remember, at first you said it was exciting, a mystery."

Nan sighed. She had said that.

Aunt Bunny nodded. "This past year has been awful. The loneliness. The emptiness. I was never so glad for summer and the Buc to come alive."

"Okay, I get that, but what's it got to do with the leavery?"

"First, let me tell you that all those things and several more I still have are yours."

"Mine? How can that be?"

"They're all things that Char gave me through the years. Birthday and Christmas presents. Friendship gifts. I loved each one, because she gave it to me." Aunt Bunny blinked against tears and cleared her throat. She closed her eyes. "Sorry. Every so often, the reality of her and Joe being gone rises up and overwhelms me."

Nan tried to imagine what it was like to lose two of the people you loved most, but she could do no more than realize it hurt. A lot.

Aunt Bunny took a deep breath. "Anyway, I chose to give many of her presents back to you, the niece she loved and the young woman I've come to love. I need to downsize, and I don't want Alana selling these things just because she thinks she can."

Aunt Bunny loved her. How could she stay mad in the face of that? "But why didn't you just give the things to me? It would have saved me a lot of frustration."

"Remember the doll?"

"Of course. It was the first thing I found."

"I planned to hand it to you, to explain that Char had gotten it for me when Alana was born, but you weren't in the store. I left it leaning against the cash register for you. When I came back later to explain, you were caught up in the mystery of it all."

Nan frowned. No wonder Aunt Bunny always had the red bag hanging from her shoulder. "If you've been leaving things, who was the kid in the black shirt?"

"That's Tim. He works the hot dog concession at the Buc. He was helping me out on his night off. He's done it a couple of other times, back before you hired Mooch. I guess Tim's now retired."

"The whole project is retired!"

"It is. Rog made me promise." Aunt Bunny grinned. "Tim'll miss it. He's had a grand time."

Nan narrowed her eyes. "So Rog not only knew who you were, but he knew it was you doing the leavery?"

"Don't be mad."

"Of course I'm mad!"

"Don't be. He was mad at me on your behalf. He made me

promise to confess. He was very stern with this old lady."

Nan snorted. "Old lady, my eye. You're a siren, luring upstanding young men to a life of deceit. First Tim, then Rog. A rich siren."

Aunt Bunny seemed taken with the appellation. "Not many women my age get called something as exciting as a siren."

"A *rich* one. You let me believe you were poor."

"I did."

"Not nice."

Aunt Bunny held up a hand. "Let me explain. Please."

Nan looked at the elegant woman. She didn't want to be mad at her. "Give it a shot."

"Thank you. It's simple, really. I was enjoying the fact that you seemed to like me for me, the little old lady with the awful clothes who lived in a little apartment with tacky furnishings." She spread her hands in a beseeching gesture. "It's a rare thing to be liked for just me. Usually, people want something from me." She indicated her elegant appearance. "This is the me they know, they expect. Maybe not quite this fancy, but—"

"I understand."

Aunt Bunny's eyes filled with warmth and affection. "You gave me the gift of liking me, just me."

Nan couldn't resist smiling back. "But what's with the apartment? You do have another house, right?"

"Joe and I started our married life in that little apartment. My father was convinced Joe married me for the Buc, and he didn't approve. Joe had been a summer hire for four years before he ever asked me out. I was in love with him from the first time I saw him, but Daddy let the guys who worked for him know Blossom and I were off limits. I'd sit in the ticket booth night after night, year after year, pining over handsome Joe Truscott. He finally asked me out his senior year in college, because he figured come June, he'd have a real job and wouldn't need the Buc. Come June he had a bride, and we lived in that little apartment. He was back at the Buc, and I was back in the ticket booth."

Nan watched Aunt Bunny's face shine as she told her story.

She wished she'd known Joe.

"It didn't take Daddy long to realize Joe might have grease under his nails because of his gift with machines, but he had a good business mind too. He's responsible for building the Buc to what it is today. Daddy soon understood that Joe was the Buc's future. Blossom married Pete, a wonderful guy, but not a drop of carny blood in his body. Blossom and I might own most of the stock, but Joe was CEO. Alana and Mike came along, and we lived in that little apartment every summer. Joe and I ran the Buc and loved being on site. Mike loved it too, though he didn't want it to be his career. Did they tell you he's a high school principal? He comes to work at the Buc for a couple of weeks every summer, sort of for old times' sake, but we all know running the enterprise isn't for him."

"Maybe Jodi?"

"Maybe. She's working on her MBA to prepare herself."

"But not Alana."

Aunt Bunny shook her head sadly. "Not Alana. She's always loved our life away from the Buc, the big house and the nice clothes. For some reason she sees the Buc as low-class, redneck, and too tacky for words." Aunt Bunny gave a sardonic smile. "She conveniently forgets that what she considers our low-class business has allowed her to live in the style she loves."

"Calling the Buc low class is like calling Disney World low-class. Doesn't she see the smiles on the faces of the people streaming in every night?"

"Joe and I often commented to each other that strangers couldn't wait to come to the Buc. Kids looked forward all winter to coming back in the summer, but our own daughter lived for the day she could leave. She didn't see the happy customers who returned year after year. She just saw the grease on her father's hands from fixing the machinery that runs the pretty rides. She hated the smell of cotton candy and hot dogs. And the long hours. Now she'd like nothing better than to sell the place."

Ah. "That's the pressure she's putting on you."

"Me and Blossom. Nothing can happen without cooperation from both of us. If I say we should sell, Blossom will go along with it. She and Pete have lived in California so many years that she loves the Buc the way most of us love the military. Admiration and appreciation and wouldn't it be terrible if it went away, but we don't want to join. Joe and I—and I think Jodi—love the Buc as a living, breathing being we want to keep healthy and strong. The Buc has given our lives purpose. Caring for it was our way of serving God."

"You feel about the Buc the way I'm coming to feel about Present Perfect."

Aunt Bunny squeezed Nan's hand. "Char would be so happy."

"I hope."

"I know."

Nan smiled. "Because you want the Buc to remain in the family, Alana thinks you're irresponsible."

"She and Jason are working hard to convince Mike and the extended family that I'm incompetent now that Joe's gone."

"You're not, not at all."

"Thank you. I don't think so either. I just need to hold on long enough to give Jodi a chance to prove herself."

Nan studied Aunt Bunny, so regal in her white gown. She searched for the homey Bunny under the glamor.

"Forgive me?" Aunt Bunny reached out and brushed a hand over Nan's hair. "Please? You're one of my favorite people. I never meant to hurt you."

There it was, the real Bunny, kind and caring. "I realize that now. I just need a bit of time to get over feeling stupid."

"I never intended that either, you know."

Nan closed her eyes. How many times did one person's actions cause unintended hurt to another?

There was a knock on the door, and Rog spoke. "You two coming out? Dinner's getting cold."

CHAPTER TWENTY-THREE

Rog had enjoyed the first part of the evening. It was a pleasure to have someone as lovely as Nan on his arm. And she did look lovely. He sighed. He might as well admit it. He was smitten.

Then came the Aunt Bunny revelations, and the evening went downhill from there.

Aunt Bunny's family had been congenial and pleasant, keeping conversation going throughout the meal and making him feel comfortable. The exception was Alana, who had been her usual snitty self, at least to Nan, with Jason exhibiting the same attitude. Rog was proud of Nan as she forced herself to be amiable, refusing to lower herself to the petty sniping Alana enjoyed. More than once he caught Blossom's distressed expression at a zinger Alana threw.

Aunt Bunny had been vivacious and chatty, clearly enjoying having her sister near. When the two women were called to the stage as part of the program, they walked up together holding hands. Sturdy Blossom and too thin Bunny. Both gave mercifully short but heartfelt speeches in tribute to their parents, after whom the wing was named. The hospital CEO and the head of Pediatric Medicine also spoke about the opportunities the wing would provide the community. To much applause, Bunny and Blossom unveiled a plaque that would hang in the lobby.

When the dancing began, Pete and Blossom rose. Bunny looked suddenly lost, her longing for her husband palpable. Rog offered her his hand and led her to the dance floor.

"I never knew Joe," he said as they moved around the room, "but I think he'd have been proud of you this evening, Mrs. Truscott. You've proven yourself a class act."

She smiled at him through eyes damp with tears. "Thank you. You're a very nice man. And my friends call me Bunny."

He felt blessed. "Bunny it is."

They danced in silence for a few minutes. Then she said, "You don't like the Ferris wheel, do you?"

He laughed. "I don't like anything that goes around."

"She loves it." Bunny didn't have to say who *she* was.

He glanced at their table, where Nan sat talking with Jodi. "She's not very happy with me right now."

"She's not very happy with me either." Bunny gave a little head shake. "I never meant to hurt her. I love her."

"And she loves you. Don't worry. She'll forgive you if she hasn't already."

Bunny patted his shoulder. "She'll forgive you too."

As the music ended, he shrugged. "I can only hope."

"It's my fault she's upset at you. You told me to tell her, and I wanted this big reveal tonight. In retrospect, it was a stupid idea."

Rog merely smiled.

He asked Nan for the next dance, and she walked stiffly to the dance floor with him. She spent the entire dance staring at his shoulder. He felt like saying, *Yo, I'm up here. Look me in the eye. Tell me what's bothering you. Spit it out. Enough of the wounded psyche nonsense.*

But he didn't say anything.

"I'd like to go home," she said at the end of the dance. He didn't argue. They waited in silence for the parking attendant to bring the car. They drove home without a word. He glanced at her several times as she stared out the side window, but he didn't say anything.

He hated touchy girls who got upset about nothing. Guys were so much easier. No sulks. It was either forget about it or fight about it. Either way, the issue was dealt with.

She got out of the car before he had time to come around

and open the door for her, which he'd done with a flourish when they arrived at the yacht club just hours before. She'd laughed at the gesture and taken his arm. Now she started for the steps to the rear boardwalk, back straight, jaw tight, wanting no part of him.

No way was he letting her go inside with that self-righteous, I've-been-wronged attitude. She'd hug it to herself all night and be a real mess by tomorrow. He stepped in front of her.

She blinked up at him in surprise, pressing her lips together. In anger? In distress?

"Okay, enough of the silent treatment." He let his irritation show. "Tell me what's wrong."

"You knew." She threw the words at him in accusation.

"I know lots of things. I knew what?" He was going to make her say it. Then she'd hear how foolish it all sounded.

"You knew about Aunt Bunny."

"That she owned the Buc? Yes, I did."

"And that she was the perpetrator of the leavery."

"Yes, I knew that too."

"And you didn't tell me!"

"I did not."

Her eyes narrowed, and she turned red. "You let me make a fool of myself! How could you?"

There it was: she felt foolish. And how foolish was that? "She promised me she'd tell you."

She stared at him. "Well, she didn't."

"She thought tonight would be the big reveal—ta-da, isn't it great?—and you'd be happy about everything."

Nan's only comment was a ladylike snort.

His anger flared. "Don't you think you're over-reacting a bit here?"

Her scowl intensified. "This is not HGTV with the big reveal at the end of the show. This was me being broadsided."

Her tone of voice made him see red. "Here's something you might like to think about before you cast Bunny and me as villains. Who was it who lied to her parents about us? 'I found my own catch.'" He said it falsetto. "'He's taking me to the gala."

She blinked. "That's unfair."

"How? You lied."

"I did not lie. I don't lie."

"Ha! We'd known each other two days, give or take, and you made us sound like a long-term item."

She suddenly couldn't look at him. "My mother—"

"Yeah, yeah, I know." What was he doing, lighting into her?

"And you went along with it!" He could tell by the righteous gleam that suddenly appeared in her eye that the thought made her feel vindicated.

"It was the lesser of two evils." When the choice was go along or call her out in front of her parents.

Her head snapped back. "Are you calling my mother evil?"

"What? No!"

She gave him an icy stare. "Thanks for a lovely evening. Don't bother seeing me to the door." She fled down the narrow boardwalk, pausing halfway to take her shoes off so she could storm away rather than tiptoe.

~ * ~

Nan let herself in, barred the door, and fled upstairs. She threw herself down in one of the chairs by the big window and stared into the dark.

What had just happened?

Tears burned her throat. She laid her head back and shut her eyes.

Lord, can I have a do-over for this evening?

How had things gone from such euphoric anticipation to this disappointment?

He thought she was overreacting!

She brushed at the wetness on her cheeks and pulled herself to her feet. She took off the lovely dress and wondered if she'd have to change the color she was painting her room because of the sad associations with sage green.

She sniffed as she pondered her partially finished bedroom. She should have stuck with the awful pink. She brushed her teeth and washed her face, taking care to remove all the mascara runs from her crying. She curled up on the sofa under a throw and finally fell into a restless sleep.

She awoke sluggish and cranky to a beautiful Friday morning, warm with the sky bright and the ocean calm. It was perfect for a summer weekend, and she was too miserable to enjoy it.

Oh, Lord, help!

She walked through the store, studying the shelves and the stock. She stopped to straighten a pile of pretty journals, angling the one on a tripod slightly to the left. She paused by the weathered wood decorative sign that read *Seaside* in large midnight-blue letters with waves breaking on a beach across the bottom. Weren't there supposed to be two such signs? Her head hurt so much it was difficult to think.

There had been three, but one had sold. She knew that because she'd rung up the sale. That left two. She frowned. Had they sold one last night, or had someone walked off with one? It shouldn't be that easy to walk out of the store with a two-foot-by-one-foot sign tucked under an arm. She'd have to check the SKU numbers when she went to her laptop. She made a mental note to put two more signs on display.

Nan continued through the store out onto the boardwalk and into the early sunshine. She grabbed a coffee and a chocolate croissant from Ed—a sticky bun was too painful a reminder of Rog—crossed the boardwalk, and stepped down the stairs to the beach, the same steps Rog had walked up the night he chased Tim, the same steps beside which he had kissed her so sweetly.

Though there were the early morning bike riders and joggers on the boardwalk, the beach was empty except for the distant figure of a man with a metal detector. Clooney?

She walked to the edge of the water line and sat in the still cool sand. She wiggled her coffee cup into the sand and took a bite of the croissant. She closed her eyes as she chewed, the sour aftertaste of last night mixing with the sweet buttery dough.

Her imagined romance was over.

Lord, I should have known better. I should have remembered Ty and the lessons I learned there about guys. It's back to my original position: no men.

The memory of Rog's voice cut through her mind—*Don't you think you're overreacting a bit here?*

She wasn't. No, she wasn't.

Was she?

She knew neither Rog nor Aunt Bunny was malicious or unkind. Both of them were nice people. Maybe she was overreacting.

But overreacting or not, they had hurt her. Aunt Bunny was easier to forgive. Trusting her or not trusting her wouldn't alter her life, but trusting or not trusting Rog could. If she didn't trust him to take her side when necessary, what future did they have? She sniffed. The answer was all too obvious. She felt even more an idiot when she thought of her fluttering heart whenever Rog smiled at her, when he put his arm around her, when he kissed her.

"You're looking thoughtful." The voice was deep and male.

Nan looked up to find that Clooney had worked his way to her while she ran on the hamster wheel of her thoughts.

The other night, she hadn't been able to see the gray ponytail hanging out the back of his baseball cap, but she recognized the kid's pail, the red spade, and the state-of-the-art metal detector.

"Clooney, good to see you." She forced a smile.

"You're looking a bit sad this morning, Nan. No trouble at Present Perfect, I hope." Clooney might look like a dropout from life, but he was too astute for Nan's comfort.

"No problems at Present Perfect." She forced her smile to be bigger, brighter. "It's a challenge I admit, but I like climbing mountains."

Clooney smiled. "Good girl." He lowered to his haunches, taking care not to invade her personal space. "I've got something for you." He leaned his detector against his side and reached in his bucket. He pulled out a long bronze-colored chain with a bronze-colored disk the size of a half dollar hanging from it and held it out to her.

Nan looked at him, uncomfortable with the offer. "Oh, I couldn't."

"Sure you can." Clooney smiled. "I give stuff to people all the time, like I gave the glasses to Mooch. Seaside's crawling with folks I gave stuff to. It's just your turn. I mean, what am I going to do with a necklace?"

"But surely whoever lost it will be looking for it."

"Not this. It was buried too deep. It's been waiting for you for a long time." He dangled it in front of her. "It has your name on it."

"It says Nan?" She looked at the disk, dangling eye level. There was something incised on it. She reached out to still it so she could read the words, and Clooney dropped the chain so it fell into her palm.

"Nah, it doesn't say Nan. I didn't mean that literally. It's a Bible verse. I don't know what that specific verse says because I don't know lots of verses, but I do recognize what one looks like. You got a Bible?"

"I do. It's sitting by the chair in front of my picture window."

"Then you can look it up." He glanced behind her and stood. "Competition."

Nan turned, the bronze disk becoming warm in her hand, and saw a teenaged boy coming down the stairs with a metal detector in hand. She looked back to Clooney, but he was already a half block away.

"Bye," she said softly. "And thanks." She looked at the disk. 1 Peter 1:2. She didn't recognize the verse any more than Clooney had. She looked at the little bronze bird that hung beside the disk. What did it stand for, or was it just a bird? An enameled letter G, smaller than a dime, also hung beside the disk. Someone's initial? Grace? Gail? Gloria? Georgia? She sighed, stood and walked home.

CHAPTER TWENTY-FOUR

Rog was at the rental place when it opened, returning the tux. Wasted money. She'd looked so lovely, but the night had gone so wrong.

If he read things right, they were dealing with intertwined issues. First, Nan was surprised that Bunny was a Buchanan. She had believed all the woman could afford was that little apartment. She was somehow offended that Bunny had money. He didn't understand that. Shouldn't she be glad Bunny had money?

He'd known who Bunny was because he recognized the name Truscott. You couldn't be in Seaside long without that name showing up for all kinds of reasons, many of them philanthropic. Nan had only been in Seaside a short time, and that time had been taken up with her store. When would she have learned what the name Truscott meant? But her Aunt Char had been Bunny's best friend. How did Nan not know?

Of course, when Nan was working here as a college girl, Char's friends would have been of only passing interest. If he remembered correctly, Nan had never even met Joe Truscott.

So Bunny's real circumstances were one situation, and sadly, he was the other. Well, not him, but the fact that he hadn't told her about both Bunny's part in the leavery and her wealth. He could see why that would miff her, sort of, but come on. The leavery wasn't even a real crime, and the wealth was good.

But the big issue was that she felt she'd been duped and made to look foolish.

He tried to tell himself that if she was that easily upset, she wasn't a good risk in the romance department. Not for a cop. How would she ever handle it if he was called out for some emergency and didn't return for a day or two or longer, and she had no idea where he was and what he was doing?

He should stick her in the same category as Lori and forget about her.

Except he had promised to paint her room, and it was only half done.

Would she want him to finish? Maybe she wouldn't want him in her house. That would be a shame, because he didn't have to report to work until four this afternoon. He could spend the day painting. If he was upstairs and she was in the store, she wouldn't have to see him or he her.

He drove to the boardwalk and parked where he had parked last night. Not that he was here to see her. He was here to get a coffee and bun from Ed's. Excellent Ed's, the woman commissioner had called it last night. He liked that.

He sat on the boardwalk bench across from the store and sipped his coffee. He should go to the back door and ring. Ask her if she still wanted him to paint. She'd probably see him in the peephole and not even answer.

He blinked and took a bite of his bun. He was pathetic, sitting across from a girl's place, mooning over her. Because he was mooning, no matter how much he tried to pretend otherwise.

He stood and glanced at his watch. It was after ten. The store was open and he could see people moving around inside. She would be busy, but too bad. He had to talk to her. He threw his empty cup and bun wrapper in the nearest waste container and walked to the stretch of boardwalk behind the store. He rang the bell.

He was surprised and relieved when she opened the door to him.

She wore her Present Perfect shirt and a pair of tan slacks, and she was beautiful even with the dark splotches under her eyes and downward tilt to her lips.

"I can paint today, if you want. I don't go on duty until four."

"Oh. Okay." Her voice was small and flat. She pointed at the stairs.

He looked at her sad face and felt like banging his head against the wall. Talk about an impersonal, unfriendly opening. Did he come to paint, or did he come to repair whatever it was that had gone wrong between them? He looked into her beautiful hazel eyes. They seemed both hurt and uncertain.

He shook his head and waved his arm as if he were erasing what he'd just said. "Forget that."

"You're not here to paint?" Now she looked confused.

He wanted her to smile, to smile at him, for him, to look at him like she had when he came for her last night. He sighed. Shavings to a magnet. He might as well face it. He was going to fight for her. He had to fight for her.

He took a deep breath. "You still mad at me?"

She looked startled and relieved. "Yes, I'm mad, but I'm more hurt."

He spread his hands in petition. "I never meant to hurt you." Of course he never meant to hurt her. He liked her. A lot.

"I thought I could trust you, but apparently I'm no better at reading men now than I was when I was with Tyler."

"Hey, I'm not Tyler."

"I know. But can I trust you?"

Talk about a knife to the heart. "You can trust me." No one had ever challenged his trustworthiness before. He was a Christian who valued his reputation for Jesus' sake. He should be mad at her audacity, but all he felt was sorrow at her sadness.

Nan shook her head. "I can't imagine what you thought when I talked about how poor Aunt Bunny was."

"I thought two things. I thought you were preparing me for the little apartment, which was thoughtful of you, and I thought you were generous and kind to treat her so well when you expected nothing in return."

"Why didn't you correct me? Did she swear you to secrecy or something?"

"We talked after I left you that evening we went to dinner at her place. I told her she had to confess who she was and what she was doing. She gave me her word she would."

Nan's face pinched as if she felt physical pain. "You figured out the leavery as soon as you knew who she was, didn't you?"

"She said she didn't realize how upset you were until you called the cops."

"You could have told me that first night."

"I could have."

"You picked making Aunt Bunny happy over making me happy."

He shook his head. "No, Nan. Not at all. Remember, she's fragile and deeply sad. Joe died a year ago, and her best friend, her life saver after Joe's death, died not long after."

"I know. I'm not really mad at her."

He took her by the shoulders and was relieved when she didn't pull away. "You're tough, Nan. You didn't *need* me to tell you about the leavery, but Bunny needed to confess. Oh, sure you'd have liked to know because you found it frustrating, but it wasn't going to make you fall apart. Like I said, tough."

"You think I'm tough?" To his surprise she looked pleased.

"You are tough. You stood up to your parents. You quit a good job to pursue your dream. You're fighting your way through the unfamiliarity of operating your own business. Tough."

"I'm scared to death I'm going to fail."

"But are you giving up or are you pressing on?"

"I told Clooney I liked to climb mountains."

He could see her anger slipping. All he had to do was not say something stupid. *Lord God, nothing stupid, please!*

"When you moved to Seaside and took over Present Perfect, you became Bunny's project. She could focus on you and temporarily forget her grief. You loved her without an agenda, a great gift to someone who usually has people fawning over her."

"She said pretty much the same thing. And I do love her. At first it was in memory of Aunt Char, if that makes any sense. Now I love her for herself. She's plucky. She's fighting for what she thinks is important. She stands up to Alana, no easy task."

"But much easier, since she has you in her corner."

He was aware of movement and glanced up to see Mooch standing in the door to the store, a worried look on his face.

"Rog," he said, "I need to talk with you."

Talk about a bad time for an interruption. Rog held up a wait-a-minute hand and turned back to Nan. He brushed a gentle finger over the dark circles under her eyes. "Forgive me for my choices? Because I really choose you." He pulled her into his arms. "I choose you."

She gripped him hard, her heart in her eyes. "And I choose—"

"Rog! It's an emergency!" Mooch looked desperate. "I need to talk with you!"

CHAPTER TWENTY-FIVE

Without breaking eye contact with Rog, Nan said, "Come in, Mooch." She stood on tiptoe and kissed Rog's cheek. She whispered, "You have to talk to the boy."

"I'd rather talk to you."

She pulled back with a smile, and he gave her that wink that always made her grow weak in the knees.

"It's about Tammy," Mooch said as Nan walked into the store. She knew it. Tammy'd broken his heart. Poor Mooch.

She stepped out the open front door to the glorious summer day. Or was it her mood that was glorious? She lifted her face to the sun.

He thought she was tough. Had she ever had a better compliment? He thought she would make it. What a wonderful thing to hear after all her parents' negative talk. And he'd waited for Aunt Bunny to speak, because he thought she was better able to bear the frustration than Aunt Bunny was to bear her unhappiness.

And he was right. Now that she understood his thinking, he was right. As for feeling like an idiot? He didn't think her one. She smiled and hugged herself.

He thought she was tough.

She reached for the disk that hung around her neck. She'd looked up the verse after she'd seen Clooney. *Grace and peace be yours in abundance through the knowledge of God and of Jesus our Lord.*

At the time, the idea of grace and peace being hers seemed ridiculous. She had been too upset. And to have it in abundance? Hah! Now it seemed not merely possible but a promise from God to her, and everyone knew God kept his promises.

She fingered the little bird hanging beside the disk. She guessed it was supposed to be a dove of peace, and the G must stand for grace. *Grace and peace be yours. In abundance.*

Enjoying the sun, the touch of the breeze off the water, and the tangy smell of salt, she felt God's grace and a sense of peace cover her. All was right in her world. She smiled at the bicyclers and joggers speeding past, at the walkers who wanted to enjoy the sunshine as she did.

A grace-filled moment of peace. Her own personal grace-gift. *Thank You, Lord.*

A well-padded, pretty lady in comfy knee-length shorts and a scoop neck tee walked to the store. Under her arm she held a decorative Seaside sign like the one Nan had noticed earlier. Rather, she had noticed the short supply.

"Can I help you?" Nan asked as she led the way into the store. She was the only staff available at the moment. Mooch was here, of course, but he was busy in the back with Rog. Since it was to be a beautiful weekend, she had both Ingrid and Tammy coming in at two to work until closing, when the larger crowds were expected.

The lady smiled as she followed Nan up the aisle. "I bought this last night, and I want to return it."

Nan had decided to follow Aunt Char's return policy, which was to give back the money with the presentation of the receipt, no questions asked, unless there was obvious damage. The receipt was to prevent someone from claiming to have bought the item when in reality they had just picked it up.

"Sure." Nan smiled. "Do you have the receipt?"

"I do. It's in the bag." She pulled out the sign and rooted for the receipt. She pulled out a piece of paper and handed it to Nan. "It's not that I don't like the sign, you know. It's just too small for where I want to hang it. You don't happen to have bigger ones, do you? I want one that's about three feet long to hang over the front door." She grinned. "We just bought our house here, and I'm having such fun decorating it."

The woman's delight was contagious. "Congratulations. I hope you and your family have years of enjoyment in it."

"It's a dream come true to have a shore house."

Nan barely heard the last as she stared at the receipt in confusion. The top of the page read Present Perfect in a font like the one on the sign over the door and on the shopping bags, but that was where any similarity to a genuine receipt ended. All the real receipts were printed by the computerized register. This one was handwritten on what looked like a page torn from an old booklet. Even the paper was darkened with age.

Nan had seen these receipts before, but where? She closed her eyes as she tried to picture their location. A flash of memory struck, and she saw Aunt Char holding the pad of receipts and saying, "I keep these in case there's a problem with the register. I'm not losing sales because I can't record them."

Nan pulled open the drawer below the register and there lay a pad of receipts just like the one the lady had handed her. She picked up the pad with a sinking feeling. She stared at the little stack of perforated edges that showed more than this one receipt had been torn off.

In a fog, she opened the register and counted out the money owed her customer. She managed a smile as she placed the returned sign beneath the counter. She took the woman to the far aisle where a pair of larger signs sat on the top shelf.

"Oh, I like that one." The customer pointed to one very similar to the one she was returning but half again as large.

Nan nodded. "Let me get someone to get it down for you." Still feeling vague and slightly lost, she moved to the office where Mooch and Rog were deep in conversation. This time she was the one interrupting. "I need someone to get down a sign that's too high for me to reach."

Mooch nodded and followed her. He looked so serious. He didn't even make a joke about her being vertically challenged.

The woman paid for her new, larger sign and left happily. She also left with a register-generated receipt. Nan opened the drawer below the register and retrieved both the woman's receipt and the booklet from the drawer. How many pages had been torn off? And when? She walked to the office with a great vise squeezing her chest.

"We need to talk to you." Rog looked almost as unhappy as Mooch.

Nan nodded. "And I need to talk to you."

"Tammy—" Rog began.

"—has been robbing me." Nan felt her eyes fill with tears. It felt so personal.

"I've been watching her, you know?" Mooch rubbed his hand over his head, messing up his hair even more than usual. "She's so pretty. Beautiful. Any guy'd watch her."

Nan nodded as she sank into her desk chair.

"I know you said no fraternization, but I could look." Mooch seemed to think she was going to yell at him.

She rubbed her forehead. "So what did you see?"

"I saw her handwriting a receipt. At first, I couldn't figure out why. No one has taught me how to use the register, but you always use it, and so does Ingrid, and even Tammy does most of the time, and it prints out the receipt. Then I realized what she was doing last night. I saw her slip the money into her pocket. I'd have told you then, but you had already gone with Rog."

Nan made a small sound of distress. Rog came to stand behind her with his hands on her shoulders. His thumbs made small circles on her back, soothing her. She rested her head against his arm.

Mooch looked like he'd taken a punch in the stomach. "I realized she must only write receipts when someone pays in cash."

Nan had already come to the same conclusion, because she could see no other possibility. "I've been wondering at the low cash amounts in the drawer each night. I know most people use plastic these days, but still, I'd have expected more cash transactions."

"I feel like a rat telling on her, but if you see something, you say something." He blinked rapidly, and Nan saw he was close to tears. "Wrong is wrong."

"What about Ingrid?" Nan asked.

Mooch shook his head. "I never saw her take anything or write a receipt. Just Tammy."

Nan felt sick. She had trusted the girl, put her in charge when she left. When she saw Tammy writing things for a customer, she had assumed it was information about a product or something equally helpful. She'd been happy to see how committed the girl was to giving good service. Instead, she'd been cleverly robbing her. Talk about being made a fool of.

Nan's throat felt tight, and she had to force words out. "If you don't put carbon paper between the pages, there's no record of the transaction. So easy. So clever. So tidy."

"So wrong." Rog's voice was cool, professional, his cop voice. "I wonder how often she did this and how much she's taken."

Nan knew she couldn't be so unemotional. She felt violated, but the thought of making the girl's actions a police matter made her stomach churn. "What will be the cost to Tammy if I report this?"

"If?" Rog raised an eyebrow.

Nan nodded and sighed. "What will it cost her?"

"It depends on how much she's taken."

"How will we ever know that? We don't know how many receipts she wrote or the

amounts they were for."

"It can't be that much, can it?" Mooch asked. "You haven't been open that long."

"And Tammy and Ingrid have only worked for me a couple of weeks."

"Say a hundred dollars a day," Rog said. "That's fourteen hundred dollars."

"That's a lot of money." Mooch started straightening Nan's desktop, his automatic response to a bad case of nerves. "You know, suddenly, being a cop doesn't sound so fun after all."

Rog smiled with understanding. "Don't worry, kid. You

don't usually have to arrest friends."

Friends. That was the problem. She didn't usually know people who got arrested either. "I know she was wrong, but I hate to think of her going to jail." A trailer of all the terrible things that could happen to a nice girl like Tammy played across her imagination.

Rog released her shoulders and sat on the edge of the desk facing her. "Nan, did you tell Tammy to take the money, or did she decide to do that on her own?"

"She decided."

"Is the money hers to take?"

"No. It's the store's money."

"And by extrapolation, yours," he pointed out. "Nan, you are not responsible for whatever happens to Tammy. She is. She and she alone decided to take what wasn't hers."

"I know, but still..."

Rog leaned forward and took her hand. "Chances are nothing more than restitution, a fine, and community service will happen to her, especially if this is a first offense. She's hardly a hardened criminal."

Nan stared at the ceiling. "It's so hard to believe this is happening. It sure puts the leavery in perspective."

"That's because you would never steal, either from someone you knew or someone you didn't." Rog smiled at her, a smile that melted her insides in spite of her distress. "Remember, you're tough. You can handle this."

She squared her shoulders. "Right." She leaned forward, and the disk that read 1 Peter 1:2 banged against the desk. Grace and peace in abundance.

Oh, Lord, grace and peace are found in You. In You. Not circumstances. Not people, and certainly not the disappointment they sometimes give. Help me remember that!

With a hurting but calm heart, she looked at Rog. "What should we do?"

CHAPTER TWENTY-SIX

Nan manned the register Friday afternoon while keeping an eye on things and smiling at customers. Her heart raced, and her chest felt tight. She took a deep breath and blew it out slowly, hoping she could act naturally when Tammy arrived.

"You're too uptight, Boss Lady," Mooch muttered as he walked by with a load of product to put on display. "Relax."

"Like you?"

"I'm Tony from NCIS, a cool dude on a case. You can be Abby."

She actually laughed. "Aside from the fact that I barely know which end of a microscope to look through, and I know nothing about sophisticated computer stuff, I don't have a tattoo." She brushed her hand over her neck. "And my hair isn't black."

"Minor issues. You can be Zivah. She didn't have a tattoo."

Nan studied Mooch. "Don't give up on your dream. You'll make a good cop someday."

"Ha! I'm a wreck. I like Tammy. Not just as a potential girlfriend, but as a person, you know? I'm acting all cool and stuff, but I never thought I'd have to help arrest someone I know. It sucks."

Tammy walked through the front door, looking lovely in her Present Perfect blue shirt, Ingrid behind her. She gave a little wave as she headed toward the back of the room to put her purse under the counter. She grinned at Nan. "I'm he-ere." She made it a three note, sing-songy sound.

"It sucks a lot," Mooch muttered.

"It does," Nan agreed. She looked at the clock on the wall, a large compass face that someone with a very large room might like to purchase, though so far no one seemed to realize its potential. "Five minutes early, Tammy. I'm impressed."

"Just can't wait to get to work, because I love it so."

Mooch turned from rearranging a countertop and snorted. "She won't give you a raise."

Tammy laughed. "Can't blame me for trying."

Nan's cheeks hurt as she smiled. She was not good at dissimulation.

"Any leavery today?" Tammy looked as if she cared about the answer, and who knew? Maybe she did.

"Nothing today. I've walked around the store several times looking."

"Do you think it's stopped?" Tammy studied the store. "Why would it stop? Not that I understand why it started."

Nan was sure it was over, but Tammy didn't know the whole story. "I hope it's finished. Whoever did it was probably scared off when Mooch and Rog chased the last leaver."

Tammy shook her head. "I still can't believe someone left nice stuff like that. It doesn't make sense."

Nan laughed. "I have to agree." She patted the counter. "I'll be in the office if you need me."

Tammy nodded and smiled at the customer who walked up shaking a snow globe with a lighthouse inside. "Don't you love it?" Tammy asked cheerfully. "It must be so cool here when it snows on the beach."

Nan lost the customer's reply as she walked into the back room. She shut the door carefully behind her and leaned against it. She took a deep breath and let it out slowly. She hated this.

"She's here."

Rog looked up and smiled, his warm brown eyes shooting her encouragement. He was standing by the previously useless security panel in the corner, talking to a man in a red golf shirt who was putting the badge that had been hanging around his neck in his pocket. Rog was in his painting clothes, so if

Tammy came into the office, she wouldn't get suspicious.

"Nan, meet Wes. He's got everything hooked up, so we have a feed from the camera by the register."

Nan nodded at him and looked at the clear picture of the register with Tammy leaning against the counter. Nan felt a sudden panic. The receipt pad had been put back in the drawer, hadn't it? She looked to her desk. Not there. She closed her eyes and tried to remember. Yes, she had returned the pad. In her mind's eye, she saw it lying in its spot as she closed the drawer.

The back buzzer blatted. Nan jumped at the sound and went to look through the peephole, Rog right behind her. A woman dressed in a knit top and carrying a wildly patterned beach bag stood there.

"That's Maureen Trevelyan, my sometimes partner." Rog opened the door and made introductions.

"Hello, Nan." Maureen's smile was warm, her handshake firm. "I'm so sorry you have to endure this."

Nan forced a smile. "Thanks."

"You've got the arrest warrant?" Rog wanted to know.

She nodded and patted her bag. "Everything's good to go. The judge was quick to comply with the request for the charge of theft by unlawful taking."

"What's the sentence for that?" Nan squeezed her hands together, trying to control her nerves. Rog, Maureen, and the tech guy looked so calm, and she was a nervous wreck. "For theft by unlawful taking?" Why didn't they just say stealing?

Maureen leaned against the desk, taking care not to topple the pile of catalogs. "Whether she's held for a third- or fourth-degree crime depends on how much she's taken."

"We don't know how much she's taken."

Maureen shrugged. "Maybe she'll tell us."

"Maybe. Which is worse, third or fourth?"

"Third. That's theft of five hundred to seventy-five thousand dollars."

"Well, she obviously didn't take anywhere near seventy-five thousand." If it were that much, Nan suspected she wouldn't feel so soft-hearted toward Tammy.

"Fourth degree is two hundred to five hundred."

Nan looked at Rog in his painting clothes, the tech with his hidden badge, and Maureen ready to go undercover. Three cops under one roof. "That seems such a trivial amount to make such a big deal out of."

Rog leaned against the back door, ankles crossed in that way he had. "Nan, justice has to be based on right versus wrong, not emotion, not even the amount. Whether she took two hundred or seventy-five thousand, she was wrong. But if you want to think with your emotions, think what would happen to her if she were allowed to continue taking what isn't hers. What does she take next time? What does she take the time after that? Who does she hurt? Who does she deprive of resources that should be available for that person's use?"

"You want her to hurt for her crime, Nan." Maureen pushed away from the desk. "She needs to learn. She doesn't have a record. I checked. Since this appears to be the first time she's tried something like this, let her get caught. Let her feel the pain before she establishes a pattern or develops a mindset that whatever she wants should be hers. The crime is minor; the consequences will not be that severe. Probation, a fine, restitution. Believe me, no one wants someone like her in jail. But she has to be held accountable."

Nan knew they were right. "You want to scare her straight." Which had always sounded good in theory, but this was Tammy. She knew Tammy. She liked Tammy.

"You're taking her actions personally, feeling her deceit is aimed at you, Nan Patterson, but she doesn't see it as personal." Maureen pulled a pair of sunglasses from her beach bag. "To her it's just money, not your money. When people steal, there's a great disconnect between taking something that belongs to another and taking something they want. Sure, they realize what they're taking isn't theirs to take, but the hurt or harm taking it might cause the owner doesn't usually cross their radar."

"Here comes a customer," Wes said, and they all watched

Tammy take the woman's credit card, run it, and hand her the register-generated receipt and neatly bagged item.

"I'm ready." Maureen hiked her bag over her shoulder and slid her sunglasses on.

Rog jerked a finger at the tech. "Wes has a great picture. We'll watch it go down. If you have trouble, which I doubt, I'm right here."

Maureen nodded and slipped out the back door. In about ten minutes, she appeared on the video feed. She had a set of four dishes with starfish and sand dollars on them, drinking glasses that matched, and pretty seashell napkins. She held up a wait-a-minute finger and disappeared from the screen. She was back in a few minutes with a framed map of Seaside. Again, the wait-a-minute, and again she disappeared. This time she reappeared with four matted watercolors of beach scenes. She and Tammy exchanged conversation with smiles, though there was no audio, so Nan couldn't hear what they were saying.

Maureen pulled out several fifties and handed them to Tammy. Tammy opened the drawer in the counter, pulled out the pad of receipts, and wrote up Maureen's purchases. She opened the register, inserted the money, and took out change, which she handed to Maureen.

For a brief moment, hope flooded Nan. For some reason, they had read the situation wrong. Tammy just liked giving hand-written receipts.

The girl pushed the cash drawer almost closed as Maureen turned to leave, weighed down by her many bags. Maureen moved out of camera range. Tammy waited a couple of moments, then looked around, her face suddenly sly. No one was nearby. She reached into the till and counted out the amount of the sale. Very casually, she slid the bills and change into her big purse on the shelf under the counter, pushing them deep inside.

"Money in; money out," Rog murmured. "Make me a copy of the video, Wes." He started toward the door into the store.

"No discrepancy in totals." Nan followed him. "She was smart enough not to take any extra."

They opened the inside office door and walked into the store. Nan hoped she wouldn't be sick.

"Officer Studly." Tammy smiled at them. She looked at Nan. "Can I still call him that even if you're dating him?"

"Oh, Tammy." Nan felt her heart break some more. The girl acted as if she'd done nothing wrong.

"Tammy Sterling, you are under arrest for theft by unlawful taking." Rog looked his most intimidating.

"What?" Tammy looked floored.

Maureen appeared at the register. "The arrest warrant." She put it on the counter. "Feel free to read it."

Tammy backed up until she was against the wall. "What are you talking about?" Her eyes were wide and scared.

"You just stole from Nan," Rog said.

"No, I didn't! I wouldn't!"

"We recorded you taking what wasn't yours to take."

"You recorded me? You can't do that!"

"Open your purse," Rog ordered.

"No! You can't go in my purse. It's private property." But her voice shook, and her face was white.

"This warrant gives us the right." Maureen pulled the bag from its place under the counter.

"You have the right to remain...." While Rog read Tammy her rights, Maureen opened the bag.

Tammy grabbed for it. "No! Nan, tell her no!" Tammy looked at Nan with panic. "Tell them no!"

"I can't, Tammy." Nan's chest hurt at the girl's fear. "You made a choice. It's out of my hands."

"Come out from back there, Tammy." Rog spoke quietly but firmly. "Don't make this harder than it has to be."

Tammy's eyes were huge. "You can't arrest me!"

"Come quietly, Tammy, and I won't cuff you in front of people." Maureen took Tammy's arm to lead her away.

"Take it back," Tammy cried. "I don't want it any more. Take it back! I'm sorry! I won't do it again!"

Maureen pulled her from behind the counter.

"Nan! Please!"

Nan pressed her lips together to keep from saying, *Stop! Don't do this*. She glanced at Mooch and Ingrid, who stood watching, faces white. Ingrid had her hand pressed over her mouth.

"She'll be all right," Nan assured Ingrid, who was shaking almost as badly as Tammy. She prayed she was telling the truth.

"I didn't know, Nan," Ingrid protested. "Honest! I didn't know."

"I didn't think you did." Nan patted her hand. "Do you want to go home?" She wasn't sure whether she meant back to her apartment or back to Kentucky.

Ingrid shook her head.

"You sure?"

"I'm fine. Or I'll be fine, especially if I'm busy. I have to be busy. I want to stay."

"Take the register, will you? And Mooch, you be ready to help her any way she needs."

Mooch stood straight. "Don't worry, Nan. We've got things under control." But his eyes looked miserable.

Nan watched as Maureen led Tammy out the back door. Rog stopped for a moment to speak with Wes, who handed him a disc. Nan felt her shoulders slump. The evidence.

Rog caught her sad look and walked to her. He gathered her close, and she clung to him as her mind spun.

"Rog, I don't want to press charges."

CHAPTER TWENTY-SEVEN

Nan sat in the back row of the small district courtroom in downtown Seaside the next morning. Her foot bounced up and down as she waited for proceedings to begin. She'd never had occasion to be in a courtroom before, and she was a little overwhelmed by the judge's bench and the attorneys' tables, so much like things she'd seen on TV. There was even a railing that separated the official area from the observation area.

Futures were decided in this room. Her foot bounced harder.

Finally a door at the back of the room opened and several prisoners, first men, then women, were led in. Tammy walked between two girls about her age, both sporting several tattoos on their shoulders and arms. One had a black eye and the other had several scratches on her face and neck. Nan guessed Tammy was supposed to be the buffer between the warring parties.

The prisoners shuffled into the row of chairs behind the lawyers. Nan didn't think Tammy saw her, and that was fine with her. She wasn't here for acknowledgement. Grace-gifts didn't require acknowledgement.

The prosecutor, a thin blond man who had drawn the short straw of working the weekend, stood to address the court for each prisoner, but different defense lawyers stepped forward, as some of the prisoners had their own attorneys.

"Robert Horton, disorderly conduct."

"Pleads not guilty, Your Honor."

"Frank Krakowski, driving under the influence, third

offense."

"Pleads not guilty, Your Honor."

One after another, those arrested within the past twenty-four hours had their moment before the judge, who frequently asked questions of both attorneys and prisoners. The American judicial system at work. Bond was set, prisoners were led away, and finally only Tammy remained.

She looked very un-Tammy, her wrinkled clothes the same ones she'd had on the day before, her makeup gone. Still, she was a pearl among pebbles compared to those who had gone before.

She stood with her head down. Her shoulders were hunched, and even from a distance, Nan could see she was shaking.

"Tammy Sterling," announced the bailiff.

"Charges?" asked the judge, a handsome woman with an elegant bob and coloring made to wear judicial black.

"All charges have been dropped, Your Honor." The prosecutor looked disgruntled as he spoke.

Tammy's head shot up and she stared at the man.

"Interesting. How about the state? Is it pressing charges?"

"Not worth it, Your Honor."

The judge nodded, studied Tammy, then pointed a finger at her. "Someone is giving you a second chance, young lady. I only hope you are smart enough to take advantage."

Nan hoped so too as she watched the judge bring her gavel down to close the morning's proceedings. As the judge rose, so did Nan. She slipped out the door before Tammy could see her. She glanced at her watch. Just enough time to get to church.

She knew she was taking a risk in dropping the charges, but she thought it a risk worth taking. The fear on Tammy's face when she'd been arrested the day before had made Nan feel sick.

When she'd told Rog she didn't want to press charges after all, he'd studied her for a moment without speaking as Wes, wise man that he was, slipped out of the room. Then Rog looked over her head for a moment, lips pressed together, obviously unhappy.

"I'm sorry," she whispered, her throat dry. "I can't."

"Are you sure?" he finally asked.

She wasn't sure. She wasn't sure at all, but she swallowed and nodded. "It'll be like a grace-gift to her."

"A grace-gift?" He spoke in a give-me-a-break tone of voice. "She robbed you." He held up the disc, proof of his comment.

"I know. I know. That's why it's a grace-gift." She put a hand on his arm. "Remember when the bishop in *Les Misérables* gives the silver candlesticks to Jean Valjean rather than have him arrested for stealing the silver he already took?"

Rog raised an eyebrow but nodded.

"Valjean was undeserving, but the grace-gift turned his life around. It allowed him to find grace and peace in abundance."

Rog shook his head in a bemused manner. "You want to be the bishop?"

"I want to be the bishop. I want to be a grace giver. I've been the receiver of grace-gifts—the obvious ones that Aunt Bunny left and many more." She gestured around the room. "This store is a grace-gift. I didn't deserve it, but I was given it. Aunt Bunny's love is a grace-gift I almost threw away due to pride. Your choosing me is currently my favorite grace-gift." She smiled hopefully at him, and shaking his head at what he undoubtedly thought foolish reasoning, he sort of smiled back. She wrinkled her nose at him. "Even my mother's concern is a grace-gift."

Nan leaned against the edge of her desk, and waited for his response. What if he fought her? Disagreed with her? Her stomach cramped and her chest felt tight.

His sort of smile disappeared. "I'd like to make one suggestion."

He looked so serious she didn't know what to expect. She held her breath.

"I'd like you to let her spend tonight in lockup."

"But—"

"Let me finish. Let me book her on suspicion of theft. Let her get a little taste of what you're saving her from. Let her hurt a little. Then the grace-gift will mean so much more."

"Like Present Perfect means so much to me because it saved me from *Pizzazz*."

"And she'll be much more willing to pay you your money back, because you'll be her favorite person when you spring her."

"But, Rog, I'm not asking her to pay me back."

He narrowed his eyes in disbelief. "Come on, Nan. Be practical here. Reparations teach responsibility."

"You're right, and they're the right thing to demand many times, maybe most times. But I'm asking for more than mere reparations. I'm asking in Jesus' name for her to live an honest life."

Rog studied her. "You don't know that she'll do that."

"I don't. Knowing it'll turn out right isn't the point of a grace-gift. The point is the giving itself—in spite of the fact that the gift isn't deserved. The bishop offered Valjean what he didn't deserve with the candlesticks. God offered me what I didn't deserve in Jesus. I want to offer Tammy what she doesn't deserve. What she does with this offer is up to her, just as it was for Valjean, just as it was for me. The bishop didn't demand anything. God doesn't demand anything. I'm not going to demand anything. Demanding a certain response to a gift makes it no gift at all."

Rog took a deep breath and let it out slowly. "Basically, you're offering her total forgiveness."

"As the bishop gave Valjean. As God gave me. It's the ultimate grace-gift, isn't it?"

He ran the back of his fingers down her cheek. His eyes were warm and his lips tipped up in his adorable smile. He cupped her face in his hands. "You are an amazing woman, Nan Patterson. Amazing."

His kiss, soft and sweet, curled her toes.

CHAPTER TWENTY-EIGHT

Three days later

"She left for the Philadelphia airport this morning." Ingrid looked ready to cry.

"It'll be all right." Nan put an arm around the girl's shoulders.

Ingrid nodded. "I hope. Her parents are meeting her in Lexington."

Mooch took a sip of his Coke. "Will she tell them the real reason she's coming home?"

Good question. Nan had been wondering the same thing herself but hadn't wanted to ask. Ingrid was distressed enough.

"She says she will." Ingrid shrugged. "Who knows?"

Nan's prayer was that Tammy would tell the truth, but things were out of her hands now. Tammy would either appreciate her grace-gift or not.

The back buzzer sounded, and Nan walked over to see who was there. Rog waved at her. She opened the door for him. He planned to finish the bedroom before going to work late this afternoon.

She looked him up and down as he came into the office. "You're looking very snazzy for painting."

He gave her a kiss. "That's because I've got plans."

"Oh." She was disappointed that the painting wouldn't be finished. She wanted to sleep in her bed, not on the sofa. "Tammy's on her way home."

He nodded. "And you're worried about her."

Nan shrugged and managed a small smile.

Mooch wandered back into the office for a collection of oblong canvas pillows sporting paintings of lapping waves and piles of shells. He pointed to Nan but looked at Rog. "She's got a soft heart."

"She does," Rog agreed. "But there's nothing wrong with that."

"Are you saying you wish she'd gone to trial, Mooch?" Nan pulled several turquoise beach towels from a box. They were thick and beautiful and a bit off brand for Present Perfect. She checked the invoice, surprised at how pricey they were.

Mooch fingered the material. "Plush. And I'm glad you gave her that second chance. Who knows? Maybe I'll go to Lexington someday to check on her." He went back into the store with his armful.

Rog rolled his eyes. "Still smitten."

"He should pay attention to Ingrid. Not as flashy, granted, but much more substance."

Rog walked over and pulled Nan to her feet. "Forget the kids. I've come for you."

"You've come for me?" The words made her heart beat faster.

"I want to take you away from here for the next little while."

"I can't leave! It's the middle of a work day."

"The kids can watch things for a bit. It's morning, your slowest time. You can spare twenty minutes." He checked his watch, then looked at her with a mysterious smile. "You've got to come."

"I've got to, huh?"

"Got to."

She felt reckless. "Let me tell them I'll be gone."

She found Mooch halfway up the stepladder replacing the large Seaside sign that had helped set off the Tammy Affair.

"No problem," he assured her. "The Ingster and I will take care of everything."

"The Ingster?" Nan looked at Ingrid, who rolled her eyes.

Three women walked in the store and browsed.

Nan smiled at them. "May I help you?"

"I've got it." Ingrid pushed her gently toward the waiting Rog. "You go." She turned to the women. "Welcome to Present Perfect. Let me know if you have any questions."

Rog reached out, took Nan's hand, and led her onto the boardwalk. Gulls squawked overhead, sun jewels sparkled on the water, and a handsome guy in jeans walked beside her. Even with the Tammy Affair dominating the past few days, Nan felt happy. Grace and peace in abundance!

When Rog turned into the Buc, which had just opened for the day, she looked at him with a raised brow. "You don't like amusement parks."

"Why don't I? Do you remember?" He stopped by the merry-go-round and waited for her answer.

"Of course I remember." She remembered everything about him, not that she was going to admit it. "Inner ear something. You get dizzy."

He nodded. "Good girl. Now, what's your favorite ride?"

That was a no-brainer. "The Ferris wheel."

He took her hand and led her to the Ferris wheel. "A super-long ride, Pierce," he told the attendant. "And stop at the top, please."

He helped Nan into her seat, and she expected him to step back so he could wait for her while she enjoyed her ride. He was so sweet to bring her here for something she loved, even if he didn't. Instead, he sat beside her.

"But, Rog—"

Pierce clicked the bar closed.

"You can't—"

The wheel started to rise.

"You'll get—"

He smiled and settled back to enjoy himself. "I took my Dramamine this morning. For you. I'll probably fall asleep in a little bit and never finish painting, but right now, I'm living wild." He looked into her eyes.

She stared back. "You took Dramamine for me?" Sometimes the strangest things sounded like declarations of love.

He put an arm around her shoulders and pulled her close. They rode two and a half circles, the only ones on the wheel, before Pierce brought them to a stop at the very top.

Nan looked out over the beach and the sparkling sea. "It's so beautiful!"

"It is."

She glanced at him and saw he was looking at her, not the water. Pleasure bubbled in her. She elbowed him in the side. "I meant the ocean."

"I know what you meant."

She felt all fizzy and full of possibilities, like a shaken soda about to explode. What would he think if she said something like, "I think I'm falling in love with you," or maybe the more definitive, "I've fallen in love with you."

Rather than risk it, she turned to the ocean and immediately felt soothed. What was it about the ceaseless march of waves that was so calming and relaxing? "Did you know it never changes?"

"What never changes?"

"The ocean."

"It changes all the time."

"Oh, it turns stormy and wild, and waves constantly break, but it's still the same sea. All the things that make it the sea are there whether it's gentle or raging. It's the same in spite of appearances. We're not going to wake up tomorrow morning and find it's become a desert or a freshwater lake. The ocean is the ocean."

"Assuming no great catastrophic natural phenomenon, okay." He fiddled with her hair,

tickling the back of her neck as he did so. "The ocean is the ocean."

"Sort of like God is God." She tore her gaze from the vast saltwater expanse to look at him. "With Him, there's no possibility of a catastrophic transformation. He is what He is, the same yesterday, today, and forever."

"'I the Lord do not change,'" Rog quoted.

"Exactly. And that's why I find my peace in Him, not in circumstances or even people, who do change." She grinned at him. "I finally figured that out."

He kissed her on her temple. "Smart girl."

She loved that he didn't make fun of her forays into theology or philosophy, elementary as they might be. He listened. He respected her. Another grace-gift.

The wheel began to move, and they circled several times. Nan took a deep, contented breath.

"We've got an audience." Rog pointed to the window of a certain little apartment, and Nan saw Aunt Bunny watching them and wearing a huge smile.

Nan waved and blew this special woman a kiss. "Love you," she called, knowing Aunt Bunny couldn't hear her but hoping she could read her lips.

Aunt Bunny sent a kiss winging to Nan.

"Once more at the top, Pierce, please," Rog called as they went past.

"Sure thing, Rog."

"You and Pierce are on a first name basis, huh?"

"We had to make our plans," he said as they came to rest at what felt like the top of the world.

He'd made plans. He'd taken Dramamine. With a happy sigh, she rested her head on his shoulder.

As they sat, gently rocking, Rog reached into his shirt pocket and pulled out an envelope. He reached in it and took out what looked like two tickets. He held them out to Nan. "For the concert on September twenty-first. I hope you're free."

She remembered the conversation they'd had they day they met.

Do you like concerts?

I do.

Want to go?

I can't. Work. Ask me again come September, okay? If you still want to, that is.

She stared at the tickets, open-mouthed. "You

remembered."

"I did. And I'm asking now instead of waiting until September. I wanted to be certain you were free. I'd also have bought tickets for next spring if there'd been any available. And next September."

Ribbons of joy unfurled in her chest.

"Being with a cop isn't easy, Nan. Long hours, dangerous situations, uncertainty. We tend to get cynical about people, because we see so much bad stuff. On September twenty-first, I might find myself called out for some reason, and the concert might be the furthest thing from my mind. It won't mean I care any less for you. It'll mean I have to do my job."

She nodded. "I understand."

"Still, I'm asking you to be mine, to take a risk on me, to accept I'll be true and trustworthy. And you can tell your parents we're together without worrying about clearing things up later because it'll be true."

She made herself look solemn in spite of the great joy that sang through her. "I have one condition."

He looked slightly surprised and a lot concerned. Apparently, he'd expected her to fall into his arms with warm murmurs of appreciation and love, and now he wondered if he'd read her wrong. He hadn't, of course, but even these few seconds of wondering were good for him, especially since she did plan to fall into his arms in a minute.

"Being involved with someone who owns her own store won't be easy either," she told him. "I'll have to work long hours, and often my hours will conflict with yours. I don't know that I'll become cynical, but I'll definitely have days that make me grumpy and grouchy. If you can handle that, then here's my condition: If you want me to be yours, then I expect you to be mine. I'll be your shop girl if you'll be my cop."

He gave her that adorable smile. "You had me going for a minute there."

She grinned back. "Good." Then she grabbed him around the neck and kissed him with all the love that was growing in her heart and bubbling through her veins. If his return kiss was any indication, he was learning to love, too.

When the Ferris wheel moved, he slid the tickets into his pocket and pulled her against his side. She sighed happily as the sun warmed her face, the sea air washed over her, and her heart sang.

ABOUT THE AUTHOR

"I love telling stories. I love the fact that stories model what being a Christian—or a bad guy—is like. Rather than telling people how to think on a subject, a novel shows the ramification of choices. After all, real life is a series of choices and consequences. I also love that through my stories I can talk to many people I will never be privileged to meet. I can share an experience with them, a visit to a favorite location like Seaside with them, talk about a deep issue with them. Most importantly we can think about the things of God together."

Gayle Roper has been in love with story for as long as she can remember whether reading one or writing one. She began her writing career when she wanted to be a SAHM for her two sons. She sold her first short story to a teen magazine for $10. The road to fame and glory awaited. Since then she's written some 50 books both fiction and non-fiction, adult and children's. All have been written from a strong Christian world view. She considers herself a novelist and teacher of writing. A three-time Christy Award finalist, Gayle has also won the Inspirational Readers Choice Award twice, the Carol Award, the RITA Award, the Lifetime Achievement Award, and 3 Holt Medallions.

SAVING JUSTICE
SUSAN CRAWFORD

After losing her brother to gang-related violence, elementary schoolteacher Kinley is on a mission to help her at-risk students. When one of them, Justice, is caught in an act of vandalism, she intervenes.

Entrepreneur Nash McGuire has gone to great lengths to overcome the poverty he grew up in. When working on a renovation project in his old neighborhood he collides with a juvenile delinquent and his do-gooder teacher.

Kinley believes Justice can overcome the influence of his environment; Nash knows the odds and has little patience with Kinley's naivety. But as the boy's mandatory community service forces Justice and Kinley into Nash's life, he can't help but discover a boy searching for love and purpose—a boy very much like he once was.

Then Justice is accused of another crime. And Kinley's stubborn belief in the boy's innocence is just too much for Nash to accept...

As they rediscover a friendship—and the sparks that never faded between them—Callum's secrets are brought back with a vengeance. How can they keep the past from destroying their future?

FIREFLY SUMMER
KATHLEEN Y'BARBO

Artist Sessa Chambers may never recover from losing her prodigal son. Even as she grieves the tragic decisions that led to his death, and left her with a toddler to raise, she's asked to work on her dream project—restoring carousel horses for the Smithsonian. But she can't do it on her own…

Dr. Trey Brown can't pick up a scalpel again. Yes, he acted in self-defense, but the events of that awful night haunt him. He was trained to save lives, not take them. When he goes to the young man's widowed mother to apologize, she's not at all what he expected. For one thing, she's not as alone as he thought—not with the fearsome ladies of the Pies, Books, and Jesus Book Club in her corner. For another, she's beautiful, and being in her presence is more jolting than any eight-second bronco ride from his former rodeo days. Before he knows it, she's captured his heart as easily as they capture the fireflies gracing Sessa's Texas ranch.

How can they overcome their past to embrace a future together?

52176974R00124

Made in the USA
Lexington, KY
19 May 2016